Tempted

Robyn Carr

Jacket design by Natanya Wheeler
Interior design by Judith Engracia

For more information, please visit http://www.RobynCarr.com

Other Works by Robyn Carr

Historical Novels
Chelynne
The Blue Falcon
The Bellerose Bargain
The Braeswood Tapestry
The Troubadour's Romance
By Right of Arms
The Everlasting Covenant
Woman's Own
Rogue's Lady

Thunder Point Series
The Wanderer
The Newcomer
The Hero

Grace Valley Series
Down by the River
Just Over the Mountain
Deep in the Valley

Virgin River Series
Virgin River
Shelter Mountain
Whispering Rock
A Virgin River Christmas
Second Chance Pass
Temptation Ridge
Paradise Valley
Forbidden Falls
Angel's Peak
Moonlight Road
Promise Canyon
Wild Man Creek
Harvest Moon
Bring Me Home for Christmas
Hidden Summit
Redwood Bend
Sunrise Point
My Kind of Christmas

**Contemporary
Single Titles**
Informed Risk
Mind Tryst
The House on Olive Street
The Wedding Party
Blue Skies
Runaway Mistress
Never Too Late
A Summer in Sonoma

Novellas
Under the Christmas Tree
Midnight Confessions

For Jim, who never gives up on me, even when I'm at my worst.
For Brian and Jamie, who love me for myself.
And, for Mrs. Traina, whose friendship has introduced me to
possibilities within myself that I had not seen.

One

*B*ev brushed her short brown hair, looked closely at herself in the mirror and decided to add some color to her cheeks. Going out. A big evening. It should make her feel better about herself. When a widow was going out it should buoy her spirits. It should mean progress. Bev felt like she was sliding back. Way back.

"I sure hope I look as good as you when I'm thirty-five," Terry, her youngest sister, said. She was pretty, twenty, and in love.

"I'm not thirty-five."

"Almost."

"Not almost. I'm not even thirty-four."

"Almost."

"Okay, almost to that, but don't rush me."

Terry smiled. "Steve's coming over. You don't mind, do you?"

"Not as long as you behave yourself."

Terry looked indignant. "Bev..." she said in a warning tone. Bev was closer to Terry than to her other sisters, and it sure was nice that Terry appreciated an opportunity to baby-sit.

"Sorry. Sure, Steve can come over. But watch yourselves. I have two little boys to think about."

"Bev!"

Beverly softened. Terry was a sweet girl. She smiled at the little sister who was not so little anymore.

Coming home was one of the hardest things Beverly had ever done. At first, she had thought it wise and strong to go on living in the house she and Bob had built. There were good friends in Dallas, the neighborhood was familiar, and the house was large and comfortable. Yet, their friends were couple friends, and Bev had learned quickly what that meant. They were good people, one and all, thoughtful and kind down to the very last Christmas card, but no matter how you looked at it, Bev was on her own.

And there were the boys. They needed a father figure of some kind. That meant one set of grandparents or the other. Bev didn't think there were fatherly role models in her family for Mark and Chuck, but moving near Bob's parents so the boys could pattern themselves after their grandfather seemed cruel... or bizarre. Bob's parents would have felt obligated to take care of her; she would have felt obligated to be wonderful all the time. Impossible all the way around.

Bev's dad was a fine man and she loved him, but he was in his late fifties now and wasn't up to much beyond talking to the boys about their sports. He wouldn't roughhouse with them the way their father had. Coming home had shattered the final illusions. They had no father. They had no father figure. They were on their own. And they weren't really home; they had only moved.

But the boys had each other. She was a little grateful now for that horrifying accident she had had when Mark was only three months old. She had wanted to kill herself at the time, when she found out that breastfeeding wasn't the only reason she didn't have her period. And that it was only one of the reasons she was so tired. Not long after she decided not to kill herself, Chuckie was born. And then she knew tired.

In the fall Bev watched Mark and Chuckie both go off to public school for the first time. The old pro, Mark, came home and told her about it.

"I'm the only kid in my class whose dad is dead," he said.

Bev shuddered. "Swell." They must have interrogated him.

"There's a bunch without dads though. Divorce, y'know."

"I know."

"What's the difference?"

"The difference is that in divorce the mother and father stop living together because they stop loving each other. Daddy loved us very much and I would give anything to have him back. Anything."

"Me too," Mark said meekly.

"I'm sorry, Mark. Sometimes I miss him so much."

"Me too."

She had clutched her little boy, the image of Bob as a child, close to her chest, hugging him fiercely as if begging for something secure, something to claim, some reason to live, anything...

"Will Bonnie have a man all lined up for you tonight?" Terry asked.

"Oh, sure. It's her duty as a friend to see if she can't rescue me from my loneliness with a stray bachelor. We're in good shape if it's a real bachelor. Some of these acquaintances neglect to mention their marriages.

But by accepting the invitation I've given silent permission to let myself be set up."

"Is it that bad?"

Bad. But Terry wouldn't understand. And she wouldn't really want to hear it either. Since Bob's death Bev had been the victim of her friends' good intentions many times. It usually was some unattached bachelor who worked with a friend, or a cousin, or a "fella from the club." And she would feel obligated to be charming for the sake of some well-meaning matchmaker. "No, honey. It's just not usually much fun, that's all."

"It's good you're going out, Bev. Bob's been gone for... well, it'll be two years...."

"A little over a year. One year and five months. Seventeen months. I wonder how many days that is." Same as the number of nights, Bev.

"You seem to have lost interest in that guy from work you were going out with. What was his name? That beautiful blond hunk..."

"Chet?"

"Yeah. What happened to him?"

"He's around. We're only friends."

"Oh, boy, I'd try to improve on that friendship. He's beautiful. Really nice too."

Beverly looked at her sister and grinned. "Yep. Heck of a nice guy."

"So? I had really high hopes when I met him. Something wrong with him?"

"Nothing at all," Bev said, her eyes twinkling. "I got a little excited myself—for about two hours."

"Well? He isn't married, is he?"

"Not exactly. He's gay."

"Oh." Terry sighed. "Oh, nuts."

Beverly giggled. She couldn't help herself. Actually, Chet was about the nicest man she had dated.

"That's really too bad," Terry said.

Yes, Bev thought. But for her, not him. She had been terribly disappointed, hurt, in fact, when he told her. She had let herself become optimistic for the first time. Chet was the marketing director for one of the department stores where she had worked. They had had several entertaining conversations at the store when he asked her to join him for a bite to eat. Later, they made plans to go out to dinner and she was frankly charmed. He must have noticed that she was beginning to feel romantic toward him. It was a very clumsy moment. Instead of graciously and quickly accepting the friendship he offered, she had delayed, feeling resentment well up in direct ratio to how her high expectations were crushed. "C'est la vie," she said at last to Terry.

"Maybe this will be 'it,'" Terry said.

"'It' what?"

"The man. Maybe this time you'll meet someone you really like."

"Maybe." But highly doubtful, Bev thought, mostly because she didn't have much interest. It was everyone else's interest that kept her going out. Like the coming-home party at her mother's.

Beverly had relented and allowed her mother to have a fall picnic at her house to welcome her home. Stephanie and Barbara, her two sisters from out-of-state, came with their husbands and babies and everyone was together. Delores didn't mention that on her daughter's behalf there would also be old high school friends and half the congregation from her church.

There were questions like: "Is it nice to be home?" that sounded to Bev like: "Had enough of being strong?" And introductions like, "I'd like you to meet John Smith," that sounded more like: "I'd like you to meet someone available." And Bonnie had been there, looking only ten pounds overweight when Bev knew it was a solid forty, who had asked if she would like to go with the whole gang to Lindy's, a new restaurant near their subdivision.

"Oh? I've heard of that place."

"There's this guy—"

No way. "I think I'd better pass. Maybe some other time."

Bev couldn't help feeling that some of those people had come to the picnic to see how much Bob's death showed on her. She had always been pretty, lively, and enthusiastic. She knew the sparkle was gone. It hadn't aged her face or packed twenty pounds on her hips, but it was there. If she could feel the weight of it, others could see it in her expression. And she didn't much want to bear scrutiny.

"How's work going?" Terry asked.

"Going, that's about all. I haven't had many calls."

"It's a bad time of the year."

"It's fine with me." She thought her job was ridiculous. She had been shopping one day, when a buyer from the store asked her if she modeled. She had never even considered such a thing. The woman encouraged her to try it by working in a luncheon fashion show. They needed more women in their mid-thirties to add a dash of maturity to their in-store shows. They hired her to walk around the store next. Then they pushed her toward an agency so they could hire her for some pictures for advertising for a sale. The whole silly thing had turned into a part-time job for which she was paid fifty dollars an hour, plus she received a twenty percent discount on clothes. Since she wasn't doing anything else, she modeled. She could choose her schedule, her jobs. But it did seem silly... meaningless.

"I'm thinking about going back to school," Beverly said. "I just can't decide what I want." You wanted to be a wife and mother. So you're a mother.

"I hope you have a good time tonight, Bev."

"Thanks, honey. It's a night away from the kids and they can use the breathing space as much as I."

"Bev, you don't think... I mean, you haven't given up on the idea that you could fall in love again, have you?"

She already had been in love again, that was one of the problems. Oh, it wasn't like it had been with Bob, but then, love came in all sizes. Guy was an old friend of Bob's from army days. Bev had known him for years. He was attractive and funny and Bev let him fall right into a routine. He was welcome in her home. He was a man in the house and that had come to mean a lot. When she saw his true colors, though, she ended it easily by moving away. He didn't cry while she packed. He didn't even say, "Awww nuts." She had come to think of it as her second bout with losing someone dear. "No, Terry, I haven't given up on the idea." Just disregarding it for a while. "Want to have a drink with me before I go?"

"A little wine maybe."

Bev poured scotch over ice for herself and a small glass of wine for Terry. She didn't really drink more now that Bob was gone; it was just one of those things she really enjoyed. A good drink. A good scotch. Her mother thought if you ever indulged it was a problem worthy of prayer. Mother might be right tonight, Bev thought, because she needed this scotch to get herself up enough to go to the party.

The "unattached male" lined up for Bev was a good-looking man about forty years old and he didn't seem to be disappointed in his albatross for the evening. He put her at ease at once.

"Do you know any of these people?" he asked.

"No, do you?"

"Most of them. I'm the only unmarried man here. I imagine it's a coincidence that you're the only unmarried woman."

"Coincidence, my eye."

"That's what I say. What should we do now? Have a drink?"

"Please, and listen, don't feel obligated—"

"I don't. For once Bonnie did me a favor."

About that time Bonnie shot a few careful glances in Bev's direction, apparently to make sure she wasn't mad, and when she was finally convinced, she came over and owned up to having played Good Samaritan. Bev learned she had told Bob Stanly that Beverly was a "nice" woman, mid-thirties, and widowed, with two little boys. Bev winced at how her vital statistics had been offered—about five-foot-six, a slim size ten with a nice—there was that word again—figure and short brown hair. It couldn't have sounded very exciting... just average, boring, dull average. She could have turned out to be a real dog. And that was exactly what Bob Stanly had said, Bonnie told her, but her husband, Phil, had quickly assured Bob that Beverly was a real looker. So good old Bob had decided to bite.

Bob was headed back, drinks in hand, and Bonnie faded away... fast. After some small talk, Bev confessed, "My husband's name was Bob."

"My wife's name was Susan. Want to tell me about yours and I'll tell you about mine?"

"Are you a widower?"

"Divorced."

"Then we don't have as much in common as I thought."

"Maybe. Susan died last year. I have the girls."

"Oh, that's rich. I have boys. I'll bet Bonnie has started sending out the invitations already."

They laughed. This was at least unique: the very first time Bev had laughed with a man over a blind date. It was a comfortable change. She was beginning to think they could be friends, talk about things. She liked his manner, his easy style. He was fun. She had a flicker of an emotion she scarcely recognized and had learned to greatly fear—optimism.

It was the little bit of snow at the temples and the tired look around his eyes that relaxed her. "I wonder if I could ask... no, never mind."

"Go ahead," he said.

"Well, I hope you don't misunderstand, but I wonder... was it so bad, losing your wife when you were already divorced?"

"I guess not," he said. He seemed to know about the gray and the tired eyes. He blessed her with a very sympathetic look that said he wasn't in love with his wife when she died. "I'm mourning my gain more than my loss, Bev. It isn't easy."

"I know," she said in a way that sounded more like a breath than words. They quickly went for another drink. A change of subject and some more anesthetic for them both.

Bob Stanly seemed safe, sober, and kind. Beverly actually had a good time. The fact that he was from Richmond and regularly drove to Columbus on business was even better. She could think about this possibility for a while. It eased some of the pressure.

The hours slipped away. It was past midnight and she didn't want to be the last to leave. Everything was very nice, she told Bonnie. Yes, Bob Stanly was a lot of fun. No, he wasn't taking her home, she drove her own car over. No, he didn't ask her out again. Yes, if he did ask, she thought she might see him again. God, but she hated the way these things ended. She genuinely hoped Bonnie would have the good sense to leave Bob alone.

"You're sure I can't drive you home?" he asked.

"No, I drove over. It's only a few blocks."

"I'll walk you out to your car and take off myself."

"Where are you staying?"

"Downtown. The Hilton."

"Wow. Expense account?"

"Believe me, I wouldn't be staying there out of my own pocket. I'm doing all right, but I'm not rich. Why don't you invite me over for a drink, Bev?"

"Sorry, maybe some other time. My sister is babysitting and she's staying the night."

"I can take you downtown, buy you a drink at the Hilton."

"Thanks, anyway, but it's late. I have to take the kids to church in the morning."

She stopped when she unlocked the car door and he held it open for her while she climbed in. She would have expected some nice, friendly farewell just before closing the door, but that was not his style. "Move over."

She wondered for a long time after why she so quickly obliged him. She moved over. "What are you doing?"

"I don't want to stand in the street and make out like a schoolboy. You can spare a kiss good night, can't you?"

She could. It wasn't obligation or conscience. She liked him. Her lips trembled. It seemed so false on a thirty-some-year-old woman. It was hardly her first kiss.

His hands slid under her coat and around her waist to pull her closer. Her lips no longer trembled. She fit to his mouth and they kissed and kissed and kissed. It felt good. She couldn't remember when she had been kissed last. Probably Guy, since Chet certainly did not like to kiss women. It was delicious, weakening.

Her arms went around his neck to hold him close. His hands were gliding along her back, caressingly, pressing her chest more firmly against his. She loved it. He leaned back and she leaned forward, enjoying the feel of his nice, lean body. It's the kind of thing you can get used to, learn to love, and find terribly hard to resist, she thought. She no longer thought of Bob or Guy or anyone. She thought only of Beverly and how good she felt, how comfortable and natural and sensual.

She kept reminding herself that she must stop him and send him on his way, but something in her went totally deaf. While he made no more demands, she couldn't bring herself to break the magic moment. Then his hand slid over her breast and she gasped in delight. She mustn't let him go further for his own good.

"No, Bob. Stop now. No more."

"Am I hurting you?" he asked courteously.

"No, of course not. Please, let's not get ourselves any more worked up. I have to go home now."

"Don't," he muttered, kissing her ear, her neck, her shoulder. The night was no longer cold. She could feel the warm blood surging through her and she wanted everything. And she couldn't.

"Stop, Bob. It's going to be harder if you don't stop now."

"Too late," he whispered, drawing her hand to his already erect member. "Come with me, Bev. You won't be sorry."

"No, Bob. Now, stop. I'm not going with you." She added a dash of firmness to her voice. It didn't register. His hands were moving and soon would find that secret place that was so vulnerable. "No. Now stop that!"

"Come on, Bev. You want this as much as I do. Come on."

"Bob, if you don't stop at once, I'm going to have to get ugly. Now, stop that."

"Bev, baby, let's just finish it here. Come on, Bev, you're a big girl. If you won't go with me, then let's just finish it here. Anyway you say."

"Nooooooo!" She shoved him against the door and slid farther toward her own side. She took a deep breath. "I don't want to battle this out. The answer is no. No, no, no! I don't want to!"

"Well, that's just fine. Why the hell did you let me go as far as I did? You ought to know better than that. What kind of frigid bitch are you?"

"I'm not frigid. And I'm not a whore either. And I don't just jump in the sack with every guy I meet and hardly know and certainly don't love."

"What's love got to do with anything? We're two adults and we could both use some relief. Grow up, Bev!"

"Oh, I'm grown-up and I can see an excuse a mile away. You can go get your relief someplace else, big boy. It's not going to do you any good to call me names and shame me into finishing you off."

"Somebody oughta teach you a lesson, lady. You're ice."

"Get out of my car."

"What does it take, Bev? You can't make me believe you wouldn't do it. What's your price? Do I have to say 'I love you'? Offer you money, marriage—"

"You bastard! Get out of my car!"

"Come on, beautiful. Let's see what it takes to thaw that ice."

He grabbed her by the arms and jerked her so that her mouth hit his hard. The gentle and courteous kissing was gone, replaced by vulgar slobbering and rapidly moving hands. He pressed her down and she squirmed under him helplessly. His aggression revolted her. He was more than ready and it didn't take an expert to figure that out. She doubted that he would actually rape her and was a little tempted to see what his next move would be.

But she was repulsed beyond that point. She fought.

She fought him wildly and he couldn't be bothered with that much resistance.

"Okay, baby, you win. You win."

It was at this point, and she had been at this point before, that she was always tempted to apologize! She held her lips in a tight line and sat still as stone while he pole-vaulted out of the car. She locked the door. She cried.

Actually, Beverly cried a lot. She just never wanted anyone to know she cried, except those select few who were allowed to know she was not made of cast iron. She had a good imagination too. Well, maybe not good, but certainly developed. She envisioned this salesman from Richmond as an ax murderer who would be sore over her reluctance and follow her home and chop her up. When she finally did drive off, she watched the rearview mirror and relaxed to see empty streets behind her. He was merely a jackass, not an ax murderer.

So this was what life had to offer widows. Loneliness, friendly homosexuals, married and unmarried sex maniacs who needed a woman and would give her a break by diving into bed with her. The dating game was definitely over. There was no such thing as a stable single man who wanted to be with her, enjoy her company. Everyone wanted her to put out... something.

Chet wanted a friend, though Beverly wasn't sure why. Guy wanted a home away from home, a woman who would make him look good and feel good. The handsome, big-time airline pilot on the make. A married or divorced woman was usually better in bed and safer than a young girl. And what did Bob Stanly want? Relief. Well, sorry, chum.

So nobody wanted Bev. Sensible, lonely, strong Bev.

How many times had she faced this? Plenty, that's how many. A lot of evenings had ended badly. A few had culminated with near rape, degradation when she wouldn't, or disappointment if she had. Well, then Bev was through. Through with matchmaking parties, most of all. Through with it all. Bev would go it alone, thank you. Alone.

Her eyes were only a little red when she got home. Terry was watching the late movie and Steve was asleep on the couch.

"Exciting evening, hon?" she asked Terry.

"Wild. Yours?"

"Wild!"

Terry made a move to wake up Steve and send him home. His apartment was near the campus, a long drive. It was nearly one A.M. "Let him sleep, Terry. I'll give you a blanket for him."

"Here?"

"Who would be waiting up for him?"

"Well, no one, but..."

"So let him sleep. I'm not worried about you. Why should I be?"

"What's the matter, Bev?"

"Nothing. Nothing, baby." She brushed the hair from her younger sister's pretty brow. She looked at the sleeping stud. Yes, he was terrific-looking. A nice, strong, lean body, plenty of coarse black hair, clean-shaven and dark-skinned. Terry had good taste. Not only that, but he was a nice guy. He was much as she remembered Bob at that age. So what happened to all the nice guys when they hit thirty-five? Were they all either happily married or sex maniacs?

"You don't look very good, Bev. Are you sure you're all right?"

"Just tired. I'm going to bed. Will Steve take you to church in the morning or do I have to get you there?"

"We usually go together. We can leave from here. Want to tag along?"

"I think I'll just send the boys to Sunday school and stay here and rest for an hour. I don't think I can handle any lessons in moral fortitude. I'm not in the mood for righteousness."

"Sure. Good night, Bev. Sleep tight."

I already am tight, she thought wryly. "Good night, sweetie. Stay in your own bed."

Bev checked Chuck and Mark, and then retreated into her bedroom, closing the door behind her. She usually left it open to listen for the boys, but with the sleeping prince on the couch she didn't want to risk the lack of privacy. She removed her pantsuit, the latest Davana design. It was good-looking. She was good-looking. She removed the very necessary bra. So what if they sagged a little? They weren't all that small. And what if she did have stretch marks? There were worse things. She had a pretty good body for someone "almost thirty-five."

She pulled on her nightgown. She hadn't worn one when Bob was alive. He liked to reach for her, touch her sometimes in the night and feel her natural cover. So why, if a guy was going to die, why did he have to give you so many lovely things to remember first? Why did he have to give you not one, but two little boys who looked just like him? So why did he have to die anyway? Why couldn't he have just stayed around a little bit longer, loved you just a little bit more?

Bob, can you see this? Can you see what's happening down here? Do you know that I still miss you, still love you? Please, I can't make it alone. Please... please come back. I can't do it, Bob. I thought I could but I can't. I can't make the hurt go away... can't make it stop... oh, please... tell God. I can't even talk to Him anymore. If He wants to make up with me, He's going to have to do something about this pain. It's getting worse. I hurt all over. Oh, Bob, I still love you, baby. I want you back... please... help me... oh, please.

Two

Bev woke up on Thursday morning feeling like a bug run over by a roller skate. She reeled from the bed to the bathroom, looked in the mirror, and discovered she looked even worse. Another miserable period.

She was bent double with cramps, her legs were trembling, her head felt like a cracked melon, she was bleeding so heavily that she was sure she was close to hemorrhaging, and she had had enough. She called her gynecologist's office and talked the receptionist into an appointment for that very afternoon to have her IUD removed.

Carl Panstiel was no stranger. She had known him for years. He went to her mother's church, had given her her premarital exam and birth control pills, checked her every time she came home to visit her parents and had cried real tears at Bob's memorial service.

She didn't see him just because he was the only ob-gyn in the area she knew, but because she liked him. Not romantic like, or even best-friend like—because he had a wife and children whom she also liked—but because he was modern and liberal in his views, clever and friendly and warm in his attitude, and because he had a real thing for her. One could almost say they had a relationship, but one had to be very careful about saying things like that.

He had a way of getting her to open up—and just now she really needed to talk. He could make her laugh. He would be sympathetic and understanding and let her pretend that that was the last thing she needed. Beverly, the strong.

When her name was called she was led into the doctor's office instead of the examining room, which was what she expected. Carl walked into the room with his head down and nose in the records that had been sent by her physician in Dallas, which was also what she expected. Her file was fairly good reading. Then he looked up, smiled and said hello, and she felt like a regular psychic.

"You want it out?"

"Yes."

"Why?"

"It's been giving me a lot of trouble. Heavy periods. It's uncomfortable."

"How long have you been wearing this model?" He obviously couldn't read. Real dumb for a doctor.

"Since Chuck was born. Five years plus."

"Heavy periods are common to the IUD. It doesn't necessarily mean anything is wrong. I can check it and make sure there's no problem or I can take it out and put in another type. There's a fairly new one I've been using that's more comfortable to wear."

"Yank it. I don't need it."

"You want to take pills instead?"

"They don't agree with me."

"The diaphragm isn't nearly as safe, even when used carefully. There's always the chance of pregnancy... a chance you wouldn't want to take."

"I don't want that either. I'm safe with nothing."

"When was the last time you had intercourse?"

So he was going to make her say it. Well, okay, Carl, you asked for it. "Six months ago or so."

"I believe you would be much safer with the IUD or pills."

Carl Panstiel, the poor deaf doctor, she thought, but she said, "I'm safe with nothing."

"You've always been a good planner, Bev. Don't mess up this time."

"I messed up once, Carl. Remember Chuck?"

He laughed, more at the sound of her finally using his first name than the thought of the accidental baby. "Are you sure, Bev? Want to tell me about why you're really here?"

"What's to tell? It's on the chart."

"Yes, it's here. 'No physiological reason for orgasmic impairment.' Is that what this visit is about, Bev?"

"No." Guy had tactfully never mentioned the stretch marks, though she was sure he had noticed. He had rather crudely mentioned the other thing that was also slightly stretched and suggested that might be the problem. She had begun to think he was right. He looked like he should be a champ, he thought he was a champ. He was a dud. "It's just this IUD. I don't need any more headaches."

"And the 'impairment'?"

"Wrong time, wrong place." She shrugged. Wrong Guy.

"Bev, are you doing okay?"

"Hell, no, I'm not doing okay. But I'm living, even if I'm not living it up. Unless you have a pill to kill that old desire, there's nothing I can do, nothing. I'm either going to have to turn into a whore, or do without."

"Are you trying to shock me?"

"Here?" Tears. Damn the tears. "I know better than that, Carl. You probably see more smut in this nice little office than I could ever dream up. I'm still not sleeping very well. Maybe a tranquilizer or something?"

He frowned. Bev knew from way back he wasn't in favor of a pill for every problem. He pushed only one kind of pill.

"Okay, Bev, let's do this. I'll give you two prescriptions: one for foam and one for pills. You know how to take them. If you use the foam once, start the pills. How do they affect you?"

"I get crabby," she said with a sniff.

He laughed. "Do you get crabby when you're pregnant?"

"I get suicidal."

Carl laughed again. He was crazy about Beverly. He always had been. She was pretty and bright. She had girl-next-door looks that contrasted delightfully with an honest personality and a wise-cracking mouth. There had been an obvious sparkle and verve about her since the first day he met her, the kind of effervescence that made those around her feel happy. She bubbled a little less now, but still there was that wit, that light and sensitive mood about her that made him chuckle. It pained him to think she was struggling to keep her chin up. She was entitled to more.

"Okay, Bev, just fill the prescriptions and have the pills on hand. If you want something else, just give me a call. Go get ready and I'll call a nurse."

"Wanna get right to the good stuff, huh, Carl?"

"I knew you hadn't changed. Nothing can change you."

"Well, go ahead, admit it, Carl. You love looking at women's bottoms."

"I admit it already. I love it."

"Yeah, but you really love it. Really."

"Yeah," he said, and smiled.

Beverly went into the adjoining examination room to strip. This was a familiar setting. She remembered all the examinations Carl had given her through the years. She smiled wistfully, recalling that first exam she'd had after she'd lost her virginity. She'd been so afraid he would tell her mother. How young she'd been. Carl didn't act like a wise guy back then. He was gentle and kind and shy with her, easing her through the procedure so she wouldn't be embarrassed.

So how could you go to a good friend, a man you liked so much, to have an IUD out when you were gushing? Because Carl might just as well be looking at her nose. He was in the bottom business. What a life. And he was a good ob-gyn, one of the best.

She checked the mirror to see if her eyes were all red from that little bit of crying. She liked her new haircut. Guy had said, "I love your hair. I love long hair on a woman. It's sexy." That's why she arranged to have it cut in one of those too-short-to-even-blow-dry styles as soon as she was back in Ohio. Because it would have made Guy mad and she didn't want to have sexy hair.

"This is going to cause some cramps," Carl was saying. "It's a little more difficult coming out than going in right after a baby."

"Is it... well, having the boys so close together and all... it's a little... large, isn't it?"

"Tighten your vagina around my fingers. More. Seems perfectly functional. Exercise will improve muscle control. Are you working, Bev?"

"Just part-time modeling."

"Modeling?"

"Don't even ask, Carl. It was an accident."

"Modeling."

"I am not a model; I'm doing some modeling. Middle-aged modeling," she muttered. "They get fourteen-year-olds to model for the twenty-five-year-olds, and thirty-five-year-olds to model for the fifty-year-olds."

"You're not thirty-five."

"Almost," she said wearily.

"You are having some heavy bleeding. Nothing serious, but if you have a problem with this later, give me a call. Don't overdo today, okay?"

"Okay."

"You have some time on your hands?"

"Afternoons. Both the boys are in school now."

"I could use a favor—"

"Carl, are you going to try to fill up my empty days?"

"Beverly..."

"Need a volunteer in your office?"

"It's the Christmas pageant at the church in Maple Hills. We do it every year. I have the five-year-olds and Sharon has the six-year-olds. She wants me to get an assistant so she doesn't get stuck with both classes. If I have a baby, you know? Want to help?"

Oh, Carl, the church won't help. I've tried that. "I'm kind of busy. There must be someone over there—"

"Now, Beverly..."

"How much time would it take?"

"Just a couple of meetings and going with your kids to Sunday school for four weeks. They'll rehearse in Sunday school, have one dress rehearsal, and then do the pageant."

"I guess I could handle that."

"If you're too busy—"

"Better take it while I'm offering, Carl. I'm not going to beg you to let me help."

"The first meeting is the Thursday after Thanksgiving in the rec room at seven-thirty P.M. Don't get up, Bev. Just lie there and let the bleeding slow down."

"Okay."

"See you in a couple of weeks?"

"Sure." But I don't have to like it.

This was so like Carl. He was probably in this with her mother. Drag her to church, let the church pull her through. Beverly had had it with church. It was not the answer. Not for her. For the boys maybe, but certainly not for her.

Beverly had to be thankful for one thing: Holidays were easier when there was family around. Thanksgiving was so hectic that she hardly thought about quiet holidays in the past with Bob and the kids. Terry, with her shadow, Steve, Barbara and her husband

and baby, Stephanie and Mike and their kids, and John all gathered at their parents' house.

Just a few years separated Bev and John, and they had been close since childhood, even skating through the teen years as good friends. And they would be close still if John weren't so busy interning at County General Hospital. He had almost no free time for Bev... or for anyone else.

It was after the enormous meal that Bev's stubbornness had borne her straight into a commitment that she and the boys would certainly regret. Her mother was discussing plans for Christmas and Bev settled back in her chair and lit a cigarette. As if it were a cue, her mother launched into an antismoking lecture. And, even though Bev couldn't enjoy her cigarette then, she wouldn't put it out. She had learned how to pretend to tune her mother out, hadn't she?

So, entrenching herself in stubbornness, she'd told her family that she and the boys would celebrate on Christmas Eve with them, but stay home on Christmas Day. Sorry, but that's the way it was going to be. Yes, she knew it was a family day. But remember, however small, she and her sons were a family. They would learn to get along without their man; they would open presents on Christmas morning without Daddy. They would be strong.

It was a lot of happy horseshit, she knew. Christmas was bound to be miserable, but what could she do? Run home every time something bothered her or reminded her of her dead husband, of her fatherless boys? Every time she got lonesome? The kids needn't be constantly reminded that their lifestyle was slightly different from others, and this was a way to show them that it could be fine, even if Daddy was missing. Bev was determined to face the fact—and the fact was that the noisier it was on Christmas Day, the less lonely it would be. Still, they would stay home.

On Thursday Bev went to the rec room in the church about fifteen minutes before the meeting was to start so that Carl and Sharon could take her by the hand and lead her around to meet all the other goodie-goodie people working on the Christmas pageant. She hated him for asking her to do this. What she didn't need now was a bunch of straight-laced devout people with whom she had to spend a lot of time through the holidays.

They became less stuffy as she spoke with them and drank two cups of coffee. When she felt relaxed, they seemed warm and genuine. She was the snob.

Charles Sullivan was the new minister and his wife was with him, Joe Somebody-or-other was the assistant minister, and Bev's mother, Delores, the big-time Sunday school executive, was fluttering around like a nervous moth distributing pencils and paper for the meeting on her biggest project of the year. All things considered, Bev thought they were making a bit much of this production, but it didn't seem to be more than she could handle. It was a good thing because Carl beeped and then disappeared before they even sat down.

"We shouldn't give Carl a job," Sharon said. "He never gets to do it."

"It must be hard. Do you ever see him?"

"We have five children. I see him when it counts. He really enjoys this kid stuff. I wish he had more time for it. Are you going to start coming here now?"

"There's a little church in Murphy that's closer. I've been taking the boys there. But they want to be in the Christmas program here, so if they want to stay in this Sunday school, I'll make the long drive. Mother would be thrilled."

"Well, understudy for my beloved husband, give the pageant all you've got. You may end up doing this without Carl, since so many pregnant women are shooting for tax deductions and all. Take good notes and I'll tell Carl what went on when I see him."

"I think I can handle it."

There wasn't much to handle. The older children would act out the Nativity and the younger ones would sing. There would be only a few lines for each class to learn and choir robes would be fashioned by loving mothers. Some decorations would be involved and Bev volunteered to do the artwork. She could have gotten off a lot easier, but she liked doing the artwork. She would be pleased to paint, and the church would be pleased to pay for the supplies.

Suddenly Beverly got excited. What did they think of the idea of a permanent backdrop for the Nativity that could be used year after year? They loved it. And what about some scene changes?

Wonderful. And some stars and things to hang from the ceiling and some portable animal figures? Terrific. And how much should she spend? Oh, about fifty dollars, but they would work on getting a larger budget if necessary.

The meeting broke up with Beverly feeling good, challenged for a change. She was wearing a not very familiar smile. It felt nice. She felt nice. Almost happy, if she dared go that far. She grabbed her coat and was going to pull it on when she noticed a man was holding it for her. It was that Joe Somebody-or-other.

"Thank you."

"Listen, Bev, I'd be glad to help you with the artwork. You don't have much time, and I can hold a brush if you'll tell me what to do."

"Thanks, I might take you up on your offer."

"How about taking me up on a cup of coffee? You in a hurry to get home?"

"No, but..." She straightened up while preparing to knock him flat. "Aren't you married?"

"No. I probably wouldn't have asked you out if I were."

For some reason she thought preachers were issued wives in the seminary. "Well, I left the kids at Mother's. I had better pass."

"How about tomorrow night?"

"For coffee?"

"Whatever. Can I call you?"

"Aren't you the assistant minister here?"

"Yes."

The assistant minister was on the make? "Doesn't that mean that you're a minister, full-fledged and anointed?"

"Yes," he said, and laughed.

"Then I guess that means coffee."

He shrugged. "If you say so. What's your number? Here, let me get a pencil."

Delores was waiting for her, but at quite a distance, Bev noticed. She also noticed her mother was pretending to be busy. That, Beverly knew, was so she could fool around with the assistant minister for as long as she wanted. Don't get your hopes up, Mother, she felt like calling out to Delores. He doesn't impress me.

"Okay, what is it?" Joe was asking. She recited the numbers. "Good. Can you get a sitter?"

"How did you know I needed one?"

"Aren't the kids you left at your mother's yours?"

"Oh, yeah. Well, how did you know I wasn't married?"

"Would you have accepted if you were?"

"Come on, Joe. Who put you up to this?"

"No one, honest. I've known your mother for a few months and I already guessed that you must be the widowed daughter with the two kids who moved back to Ohio." He shrugged. "That's it."

"Humph, I'll bet. We aren't going to go out compliments of the collection plate, are we?"

"The church pays my salary, Beverly."

"Then we'll go Dutch."

"Beverly..."

"Dutch or nothing."

"Okay, I was just going to tell you that I have an outside income. I'm a referee with the city league. Youth basketball. I could make sure I take you out on that salary."

"Why do you want to take me out at all?"

"Why not?"

He certainly didn't make it easy to refuse. Such innocence mingled with guile. Well, at least he wouldn't try to rape her, she could be reasonably sure of that. Did ministers get turned on? Doubtful. Did they drink? No. What did they do? Paint scenery for Christmas pageants, drink coffee, and save souls. Oh, Beverly! How stupid can you be? He's going to want to save your poor lost soul. How are you going to get out of this one? That was the question she was asking herself as she and Joe said good-bye.

Delores moved in then and in championship mother style extracted the news of the date from Bev. Delores quickly grew feverish with happiness. He was such a nice young man, so good-looking. He came to Ohio for this assistant's position and would very likely be getting his own church. He wasn't married, of course, but a nice man like that wouldn't be single for long. And he loved children, especially boys. Oh, and the boys were going to love him, too—

"Mother! I made a date for coffee. Now, stop it before you get so worked up you'll be a candidate for a heart attack."

"It's just what you need, Beverly, to get together with a nice man like Joe."

"I'm not getting together with him. I'm having coffee with him. That's all."

"He has such a good outlook on life. He's been organizing sports for the young boys in the church."

Probably just another funny-bunny. "That's great, Mother. Now forget about him."

"Why should I forget about him? I'm glad he asked you out."

"He didn't ask me 'out.' We're just going to talk about the program."

"Well, that's a start—"

"Mother!"

"Beverly, I can't help myself. I'm happy that you're interested in a good Christian man like Joe, dark and..."

Oh, Lord, Beverly thought, her mother had no tact whatever. Getting interested in a good Christian man was not one of Bev's goals. She had been looking for a way to live without a man. She wanted to stop thinking about what to do with some man's clothes when he died, or how to scrape his image away from a home shared and loved with him. She wanted to stop wondering who would help her cut the grass, act like a father to her sons, and hold her when she cried. Looking for someone had been painful. Whether he was a Christian or a heathen wouldn't make it any easier when a man let you down... or just died. Bob had been a good Christian man.

Beverly had been a Christian.

Even now she prayed, but for something to believe in. She had decided there was no God. Or, if there was, He was indifferent and careless—and she didn't want to put her faith in one like that.

There was a time when her faith had healed her spirit, given her hope, and added courage to her optimism. It strengthened her determination to be morally strong and decent. In raising children one couldn't just show them the world and let that guide them. She had introduced them to religion and hoped that the moral teachings of the church reinforced her efforts to help them grow into good men. She wouldn't mind if they believed there was some Divine reason for their sufferings, but she could no longer accept that.

When she was mourning Bob's death, Delores had said, "I believe there is always a reason for these things, however hard it is to understand."

"Good, Mother. You believe that if you want to," Bev had said, but she thought that no loving, caring God would kick a man when he's down.

Just the same, Beverly tried to put that minister together in her mind all the next day. She had Terry come to baby-sit and stay the night, but the eager-beaver preacher hadn't even called. Finally, at about five o'clock, he did.

"Hi, Bev. This is Joe."

"Hello, Joe. How are you?'

"Fine. About tonight. Let's make it seven and I'll take you to dinner. I'll treat... on my ref's salary."

"I don't know, Joe. Maybe we better just stick to that coffee date."

"Why? Do you have other plans?"

"No, no, it's not that. Aren't your finances rather... limited?"

"Yes," he admitted with a laugh. "After I have you eating out of my hand I'll just take you to the park or something on our dates."

"I think I'd rather have coffee."

"Put on something terrific. Something feminine. I'll take you to a great place tonight and tomorrow night I'll just take you for a ride."

"I don't recall you asking me to go steady, Reverend. In fact, all I remember is that you asked me out for coffee."

"Okay, we're having our coffee at the Marquis Lounge. Wear something slinky. See you at seven."

"Joe? Joe?"

Well, damn. He didn't even ask how to get to her house, she fumed. Now what? And he thought she was so easy that he didn't even have to ask for a second date. Slinky? What was this slinky business? He was a minister, for Christ's sake. Well, something like that.

Three

"I can't imagine what he's thinking of," Bev told Terry. "I didn't think ministers took their dates to places like the Marquis Lounge. I thought they took them to PG movies and ice cream parlors."

"Well, he's only a man, after all. What are you so nervous about? He's a nice guy."

Nice guy. Red alert. Nice guys hurt. And not always on purpose. "I don't think we have very much in common."

"He's easy to get along with. He heads up the youth program at church. The kids really like him."

"Why?"

"Because he's with it, I guess. For a preacher, he doesn't spend much time preaching. The kids talk to him."

"You? Do you talk to him?"

She shrugged. "I don't have anything to talk to him about."

"Well, religion. You're pretty religious, aren't you?"

"I have so much going on at school, Bev, that I'm doing good just to make it to church most Sundays with Steve. But I like Joe. He's a real nice guy."

Look out, here comes another real nice guy. "Well, I hope we don't have a terrible time. I hope we don't discuss religion."

"What's the problem? You were practically raised in that church. At least you're the same religion."

"Only a little."

"What do you mean 'only a little'?"

"Well, I go. I haven't burned my membership card, but I don't believe."

"That's crazy."

"Is it?" Bev turned to show Terry the hard glint in her eyes. Terry was the only one Bev purposely spared, but not this time. Now she let her mind focus on Bob's suffering before his death, then the misery of clearing his presence from the house they had lived in together, finally her fears and strain raising his sons alone. The blue of Beverly's eyes was usually alive and bright in spite of all she'd been through, but when she allowed herself to feel that pain, her gaze was lost someplace miles away. Hard and distant. It was no joke.

Terry swallowed hard. "Why bother even going to church then?" she asked softly. "Why get the boys all involved and everything?"

The question brought Bev back to herself. Mention of the boys usually did. Facing up to the hard truths in life was painful; she could almost get lost in the pain. However, she was more of a caring mother than a bereaved widow, a feeling that very often saved her life. "Because I'm not opposed to religion, Terry. And there's nothing wrong with faith that makes people strong. The boys shouldn't be deprived of that." And a little because Bob would have wanted it that way.

"There's the bell," Terry announced as if Bev had suddenly become stone deaf.

"Let him in, will you?" Bev called as she raced for her room. "I'm going to brush my teeth." And put on the finishing touches. She heard Terry as she reached the bedroom door.

"Mark and Chuck, this is Reverend Clark."

"Joe. Just call me Joe. Where's Beverly?"

"Getting ready. She seems to be a little nervous."

When Beverly glided back into the living room, Joe was smiling. His smile went very well with his tanned face and sandy-colored hair. It was bright and wild. Even sexy, if you could say that about a minister without being condemned.

Beverly had obliged him in the slinky department. The jump suit was even a little more than slinky; it simply drooled over her long, slim limbs. She had unbuttoned a few buttons to allow her cleavage to show. As if that wouldn't be enough, she had decided on a necklace that would bring attention to her assets. And dangling earrings against her super-short hair. Plus plenty of makeup.

Terry was staring with wide, horrified eyes. And Bev could read her mind: what are you doing, Sis? Trying to scare him away?

She was right in style for Joe Average, but how was Joe Preacher going to respond, Bev wondered.

Joe Clark smiled.

"I think I'll have a drink before we leave, Joe," Bev announced smoothly. "Will you join me?"

"What are you having?"

"Scotch on the rocks."

"Fine. Put some water in mine."

Terry choked. The whole world was falling apart. Joe lit Bev's cigarette and, as she took the first long drag, Terry wanted to disappear into the wall. She was astounded. Crazy, the whole world must be going crazy when ministers asked for water in their scotch and lit cigarettes for their dates.

"I made reservations for eight o'clock, so let's not waste too much time. Did you tell Terry where we'll be?"

"I wrote the number down, Terry. By the phone. Call me if the boys give you any trouble."

She handed Joe his drink and he took one swallow, two, thank heavens he didn't take three. He held the glass away from his face and studied the amber fluid. He was catching on.

"Is your drink okay?"

"Fine." He went directly to the water faucet. She wasn't fooling him a bit. "A little strong."

Terry whirled away, unable to take anymore. The whole world would go up in smoke if Beverly didn't stop trying to bait a man of God. Beverly must be losing her marbles.

"You don't drink?" Bev asked Joe.

"Not often."

"That means sometimes," she decided aloud.

"It could mean that."

It could mean he didn't buy drinks. "Good scotch," she hummed, sipping.

"It's okay."

"You don't like it?"

"I'm not wild about scotch, no."

"Then why are you drinking it?"

He smiled mischievously. "So my mouth will taste like yours. Don't overdo it, Bev. I'm not scared of you."

Oh, yeah? We'll see. "Will I have to drive you home?"

"I hope not. Are you about ready?"

Whenever you are, preacher baby. "Yes, shall we?"

Joe went to say good-bye to the boys, who were parked in front of the TV. He looked very unlike a man of the cloth in his tan pants and dark green sport coat. No tie, of course, and the top two buttons of his shirt were unbuttoned. She noticed a froth of hair on his chest, and then hated herself for noticing that. He was real sharp, as a matter of fact. Shouldn't he be giving all his money to starving children instead of going around looking sharp? At least he didn't wear gold chains. That would be too much. But he didn't need them tangled up in his chest hair. And he was quite tall, a little over six feet. Not that she cared.

He tousled Chuck's hair and gave Mark a pat on the head. Bev checked eyes with Terry. Oh, very, very cold eyes. She was warning her. Don't you hurt him. He's a nice guy. Bev's warning system went off. Nice guy. Red alert.

They walked out to the car. Did the congregation buy the car too? She felt a little less safe with him. There weren't any people around to keep him from belting her. But then, would a minister belt a lady? No more than one would drink.

"Cute kids," Joe said. "Real tough little guys. Do they like basketball?"

"They seem to like all sports."

"Can I take them to the gym tomorrow?"

Bev's head shot up in surprise. "Why would you want to do that?"

"Why wouldn't you want me to?"

"But you don't even know them. They might be real monsters for all you know. Little devils."

"I'll be surprised if they're not. Is nine o'clock too early? I have some things to do in the afternoon."

"If you're sure." She shrugged. What is this? Is he trying to get to me through the kids? Bev stiffened. It wouldn't be healthy to enjoy this too much. It wouldn't be safe to start to really like him, trust him. Remember, Bev. Remember Guy.

Guy had been the worst. Beverly had started to love Guy in a fashion. Or at least she wanted to love him. He was handsome and kind and financially secure. He took her to fancy places and seemed genuinely proud to have her as his date. He played with the children. He gave her plenty of time to adjust to the taste of his mouth and the feel of his hands. After a long time and many oaths of love she invited him to her bed. Zero. Well, she was nervous, like a new bride, not knowing what he would expect and how he would react. She invited him back. Ditto.

Then he obviously felt he was home free. No more nice evenings out. Steak on the grill and Beverly's booze. Get the kids to bed early. Pick me up when my plane arrives. What's for breakfast? Cut the grass? You can afford lawn service, can't you? Marriage? We have everything we need right now.

Bev tried to discourage him, but Guy was so comfortable in her home that he didn't notice her displeasure. He was very much at ease in Bob's place. Whatever problem she had with getting her satisfaction, well, that was her department. She had to get her head straightened out. You know, the widow thing. Not really ready for another man or something. Bunk.

"I'll come by for them at about nine o'clock and we'll just shoot some baskets and horse around. They'll be home by one."

"Thanks, Joe," she said with an unexpected attack of politeness. "They need someone to horse around with. Since Bob died there hasn't been anyone to play with them that way."

"How did Bob die?"

"Mother didn't tell you?"

"I didn't ask. Would you rather not talk about it?"

"I don't mind. He was in an accident. Car-truck. He was just starting back from Kansas City. He had been there on business."

"Very sudden?"

"No, unfortunately. He lived for three weeks. Three very painful weeks. Mom had to fly to Dallas and take care of the boys and I had to go to Kansas City and stay with Bob. It was very slow. He had seven operations and died during the last one."

"Was he conscious?"

"Only a couple of times. One of those times when he realized I was there and tried to talk..." Her voice caught. She would never forget that. "He was hurt everywhere. I don't think one part of his body was uninjured. Brain damage, internal injuries, kidney damage, spinal damage, broken bones I couldn't count. He was in constant pain. It was cruel that he lived that long. Had he lived any longer..." She shook her head. She had prayed for his death. Now she prayed for his return.

"Jeez, that's awful. You must have had to be very strong through that. A lot of people would have folded their hands."

"What makes you think I didn't?"

"Did you?" He turned and looked at her across the front seat with one eyebrow raised as if he knew the answer.

"No." Beverly the strong. "You get through it if you have to." She didn't look at him. Strength was no gift. Hundreds of times she wanted to be able to lay her head down and die. Thousands of times she screamed silently at fate for taking Bob and leaving her to carry on alone. A million times she thought about getting drunk and taking a handful of pills and before the ice would hit the glass a little voice would say, "What'sa matter, Mommy?"

"You didn't buy your supplies for the Christmas program yet, did you?" Joe asked.

"Not yet. Why?"

"If you want me to go with you and help you cart the stuff over to the church, I'll be glad to do it. Just give me some notice."

"I might have to find a truck. I'll let you know."

"I have a truck."

Naturally. He had everything and knew everything and was nice besides. Sometimes Beverly was just plain unlucky. It wouldn't be hard to give a bastard a toss, but a nice guy? Dammit.

"Okay, Joe. I'll give you a call next week after I have a look at my schedule. I don't think I'll be working much."

"You're working?"

"Well, not exactly. I'm sort of... a volunteer."

"Oh, about tomorrow night, how would you like to go with me to a dinner party? The hostess said I can bring a guest and I have to put in an appearance at least. I believe you know the—"

"Now, look, Joe. I don't know where you got the idea that I want to go out with you every night, but I don't. I don't want to spend every free minute with you. I have other dates too. Okay?"

"Okay. So about tomorrow night, I'm going to the Panstiels, and as far as I know—"

"No."

"Okay, then how about putting on some coffee and I'll come over after?"

"Don't you have any friends?"

"No."

"Okay. Coffee. And don't press your luck."

It wasn't far to the restaurant. Joe helped her out of the car and held the door open to the Marquis Lounge. He had a table reserved away from the blasting music in the lounge. Bev was relieved because the noise from the rock band interfered with her digestive tract, but she was not encouraged by the idea that he might hope they would talk.

They were greeted first by a cocktail waitress and Joe asked Bev if she would like another drink. Actually, he did not emphasize another, but she got that strange gleam in her eye that said if he was counting, she was drinking. She ordered a scotch. He ordered a cup of coffee.

Beverly hated self-righteous people. She hated puritans. She had had it with ministers that were about thirty years old and— thirty years old?

"How old are you?" she asked him.

"Thirty."

"God."

"How old are you?"

"I'm older than you."

He wasn't old enough to look at her as if he could see into her soul and couldn't wait to get in there to straighten it out.

"Why aren't you married?"

"Why aren't you?" he countered.

"I was," she cried defensively.

"I wasn't. Haven't met the right woman, I guess."

"Too many years at the seminary, probably."

"I don't think that's it. It's not considered bad form to fall in love."

They ordered dinner and Beverly ordered another drink. Her head was beginning to spin and Joe had his coffee refilled.

"You don't want another drink?" Nuts. Her words were already starting to run together. It wouldn't be very long before the preacher across the table was only a blur. That was one way to make him go away.

"No, go ahead. I'll see that you get home."

The nerve. As if she couldn't hold her liquor. She would show him. She ordered another drink to go with her dinner. Damn preachers.

Of course they didn't talk much. He was getting more coffee and she was getting more scotch. He was looking into her soul and she was getting drunk. He was laughing in his fist and she was trying to sit up straight. He was beginning to hope she wouldn't mess up the car and she was hoping for the same.

Beverly didn't eat much dinner. It wasn't even ten o'clock before they took the last of it away.

"Dessert?" the waitress asked.

Unthinkable. "No, thank you," said Beverly.

Joe looked her over. "None for me either," he said considerately. "How about a cup of coffee, Bev?"

Over my dead body, preacher boy. "I believe I'll have another sotch... um, scotch. If you don't mind?"

He looked straight at her. "Go for it." And to the waitress, "Bring me a brandy and the check, please."

"Will we be leaving right away?" she mumbled after he had signed the credit card slip for the dinner.

"I think so, Bev. I don't think you can take much more."

"Why, whatever do you mean, Rev-rend? I'm having a wonderful time."

"Yes." He laughed. "I can see that. Do you want the rest of that drink?"

She held her lips in a tight line and nodded. He wasn't going to rush her. She finished her drink leisurely. He watched. She didn't talk. She was drunk as a skunk and wasn't about to open her mouth and prove it. She had had very little to eat all day and the booze was taking its toll. He was probably counting scotches. He probably thought he would have to help her walk out.

He did. The minute she stood up she sat down again and once she got into the cold night air her head went wild. She could hardly put one foot in front of the other. Beverly yielded the game. She lost. She wouldn't be a sore loser on five scotches. She was a rather fun loser.

"Okay, you win. I'm in the bag. Just get me home before I pass out."

"I'm glad I picked a close restaurant. Did you have to get drunk to go out with me?"

"Didn't have to, Rev. I like to now and then. See, I'm not your type. You need a sweet little girl you can take to the church socials."

"Church socials?" He hooted. "They still having church socials around here?"

"Well, sure. I'm not the church social type. I'm more the convention type. I used to go to conventions with Bob. You ought to go south, you know? Get a nice little southern belle to take to the socials. Leave the convention dollies alone."

Joe laughed harder. "Come on, Bev."

"Ever seen someone good and drunk, Preach?"

"It's been a while."

"A southern belle wouldn't drink. Well... an occasional mint julep ... or a little cooking sherry. But she'd be straight for the social; you could count on that. Good little preacher's wife."

"I don't recall asking you to marry me, Beverly. Have you already refused?"

"Yesh, I decline, thank you very much. And I decline to go to bed with you too. You see, even though I am the 'merry widow,' I do not have to go to bed with anyone. I can if it pleases me, but I will say no. Do you understand? The answer is no."

"I understand."

"Well, good. Have you ever kissed a woman, Reverend?"

"Yes, Beverly."

"No, I mean really. Really kissed a real woman?"

"Yes, Beverly."

"Bull."

Joe pulled the car off to the side of the road. Poor Terry. He hated to take Beverly home in this condition. Terry wouldn't be used to this. This was just a game Bev was playing. Running. Hiding.

"Why are you stopping?"

He pulled her to him and kissed her in the most passionate and feverish way he could under the circumstances. So, a man of the church wasn't supposed to feel. Well, Beverly, feel this. He moved on her lips and pressed her body close. He massaged, rotated on her mouth. Perfect fit. Amazingly, the perfect mouth for his. Uncanny. Her lips parted and he couldn't resist the urge. Scotch. He'd have to get her off the scotch before next time. He clung and she whimpered. He caressed her back and she moaned softly in his arms.

Dirty trick, Bev. Drunk or not, she was tempting. A little too tempting. Joe felt his desire spiral. Live with it, Joe baby. She was too drunk to notice. She would probably forget all this anyway. She curved a little bit more with desire, definitely asking for more. His hands moved under her coat. She hadn't even buttoned her coat. He had to let his lips rest to see if he could think any more clearly when he wasn't tasting her mouth. He couldn't. He went back. He found a tempting breast, he found the buttons, and he found his good sense. He broke away.

"Okay, Bev, let's get you home."

"Home?"

"Home."

"But—"

"The answer is no, remember?"

"What's the matter, Reverend? Conscience getting to you?"

"Yep."

Beverly began to cry. Drunk tears. She made a fool of herself. A complete ass. If he had thought anything of her in the beginning, he sure didn't now. Now she had spoiled it and that was that. Now he wouldn't be hanging around the "merry widow's" door, playing with her kids, saving her soul, and delivering her home after a good drunk. Well, fine. Now she could just go it alone.

"Come on, Bev. We're home."

Sniff. Sniff. "I don't want Terry to see me like this."

"Well, you should have thought of that on your third or fourth scotch. It's too late now."

He had counted. "I can't."

"Come on!"

"I can't."

"Dammit, Beverly, come on!"

"Okay, okay. Help me a little here."

It took more than a little help. It took a lot of help and the sidewalk was slippery besides. Joe had to ring the bell because Beverly couldn't find her key. She wasn't even sure she had her hand in her purse.

"Beverly," Terry began, confused. "What's the matter?"

"Make some coffee, Terry. Beverly's drunk."

"Drunk? Oh, Beverly, how could you?"

"Scotch," she whined.

"Okay, Bev, I want you to go take a shower and then have some coffee."

"All alone? Aren't you going to help me, Joe?"

"Maybe some other time. Go on now."

"Bye-bye, Joe. Thanks... for everything."

Beverly hummed on the way to her room. She might not know it now, but the minute she started pulling off her clothes she was going to be sick. Joe knew it.

Joe found a seat in the living room. Comfortable little place she had. Domestic. Nice kids, nice sister. Joe had a sweet little sister once. Terry made him miss that sister even more.

So, this was the house of Beverly. She would have painted the pictures on the walls. She liked rust and gold and orange. A little green. Basically warm and open colors; fall colors. People who liked the fall liked the bright crispness outside and the warmth inside. The brightness of hillsides intensified with the fire in the hearth. That was Beverly. Crisp and sassy on the outside, warm and friendly on the inside. When she wasn't so scared.

Beverly was still humming in the bedroom. Joe wouldn't put it past her to stroll naked into the living room. He hoped to take in such a sight any other time. Right now he was feeling a little too sensitive.

The shower was running when Terry came out of the kitchen nervously wringing her hands on a dishtowel. "I'm really sorry, Reverend Clark. I don't know what got into her. She's never done anything like this before... that I know of."

"I know, Terry. It's all right."

There he goes with that smile again, Terry thought. No wonder Bev got drunk. It was that gorgeous, suggestive smile that drove her to it. "You're taking this pretty well."

"No big deal. It happens to the best of us."

"You?"

"Well, not since the army."

"Why didn't you cut her off?"

"Because she wanted to get drunk, Terry."

Oh, brother. So we just let her do whatever she wants to do now, whether we like it or not. Holy tolerance.

"Were you planning on staying over?" Joe asked.

"Yeah, I always do."

"Good. Check on her, will you? After she's out of the shower, see if you can get her to drink some coffee. It might make the morning easier."

"You think she'll be hung over?"

Joe laughed. "Bad," he said simply. He stood, took a last look around the pleasant living room, and then headed for the door. "Why don't you get the boys up in the morning and let Bev sleep in. I'm coming to pick them up at nine o'clock for a trip to the gym with me. Bev said it was okay."

"You're going home now?"

"Sure. She's not going to want to see me when she starts her hangover. See you in the morning."

"Okay, bye, Joe."

Joe stepped out into the cold night. Okay, Beverly. I think I know what you're up to. You're so afraid you'll feel something like love again, you can't even think straight. Well, take it easy, baby. I'm not going to rush you.

Take a deep breath, Joe old boy. There, you're doing fine. Hold on to your hat, you're going for a real ride. Charge up God's chariot. How long has it been? A year? Two? Father, I need a lesson, I need a loan. I need some restraint. Patience, common sense. I need a woman like Beverly. I need a drink. Amen.

Four

Terry's alarm could have awakened the dead, she thought as she dressed, yet there wasn't a sound from Beverly's room. She roused the boys and asked them if they wanted to go to the gym with Reverend Clark.

"That Joe guy?" Mark asked.

"Yes."

"What for?"

"I forgot to ask him. Just get dressed and we'll ask him when he gets here. He said nine o'clock and it's already eight-thirty, so hurry."

"I hate going with these weird guys," Mark said, pouting.

"What weird guys?"

"Whenever some guy likes Mom we have to go play with him until she starts to like him back and then we can stay home and watch cartoons."

Nothing got past kids, Terry realized with dismay. Poor Bev. Terry hadn't really thought about how awful it must be at times. Doling out her children like favors to the men who wanted her attention. And when did she know genuine interest from a big play? And what was she supposed to do? Deny the boys the opportunity to have the companionship of a man?

Terry decided that she would have to call John. This was his responsibility, no matter how busy he was. He would have to see about his nephews a little, start hanging around to be their man. They needed someone who wouldn't abandon them. And an uncle was better than a would-be suitor of their mother's. Bev must be too proud to ask.

Joe was at the door about ten minutes early, sweat pants and tennis shoes on the bottom half and a heavy ski jacket on the top half. He was smiling that smile again. It made Terry a little uncomfortable. He was too sexy to be holy. He should be out sowing his wild oats with other men his age.

Joe accepted a bowl of Wheaties to eat with the boys. Didn't have time for breakfast, thanks, was his reply. "Is there any of that coffee left, Terry?"

"Some. The dregs, I think. It's going to be a little stiff."

"That's okay. Heat it up for me, will you, and then make a fresh pot for your sister. How is the grande dame?"

"She wasn't too well last night. I haven't heard from her yet this morning." Then, in a whisper for Joe's ears only, she added, "Boy was she plastered."

Joe surprised her with a laugh. "She'll pay for it. That kind of fun doesn't come free."

"Fun? You think she had fun?"

"For a while she had a great time. I could hardly drive, she had me laughing so hard. Didn't she tell you she had fun?"

"No," Terry murmured, hiding her eyes.

"Done, Chuck? Go brush your teeth and get some tennis shoes for the gym. And some shorts. You too, Mark. Is it coffee yet, Terry?"

"Coming up. How's that for service?"

"What did she say, Terry?"

"She was a little depressed."

"A little depressed?"

Terry was going to cry herself if he pushed her. Joe could see the struggle. Bev was not a little depressed. She was probably a complete wreck. Choking and wailing. Ready to quit.

"I'm worried about her, Joe. I think she's had about all she can take. She wants everyone to think she's strong, tough. I don't think she really is. I don't know how much... and the boys—"

"What about the boys?"

She repeated what Mark had said. "It figures," Joe commented. "Well, if it makes you feel any better, my taking the boys has nothing to do with Bev. I usually take some kids to the gym on Saturdays. I like kids. Always have."

"I know, Joe. I'm not accusing you or anything."

"Just because I preach for a living doesn't mean you have to trust me, Terry. I'm just a human being. I want to be a good one, but mostly I'm just another man. I'll see what I can do about Bev."

"Um, Joe?"

"What?"

"About Bev, well, she's decided she doesn't believe in God anymore. She used to pray, Joe. She and Bob always went to church and she was rather proud of that."

"Oh?"

"Just 'oh'? I told you she doesn't know God anymore. Isn't this your area of expertise?"

He shrugged. "Maybe I'll introduce her sometime."

Oh, Bev wasn't going to like that. "I shouldn't have said anything."

"Did you think I wouldn't find out? Come on, don't worry about it. Lots of people lose faith and stumble along. Bev hasn't lost God; He still believes in her. She's just lost direction and is a little short on perspective right now. She'll be needing someone to help her out with that."

"I wish I could."

"I think it's better if it's me, Terry." Joe smiled and patted her on the head. "Especially since it's probably going to make her mad. Besides, don't you have a Steve somebody to worry about? Can't you just leave Bev to me for a while?"

Terry studied Joe's face. "Terry," he said with grave seriousness. "She'll be safe. And I want to."

She nodded just as the boys were running to the front door while pulling on jackets. She watched as Joe and the boys went out to the car.

Joe started the whole thing. He flung the first snowball and he got them going. It took nearly as long for them to get to the car as it did to eat breakfast. Joe called a truce on the snowball fight, two against one, no fair. He wouldn't let them get into the car, the church's car. He pulled a blanket out of the back and spread it across the front seat. Then they all got in and drove away.

"Come on, God," Terry prayed earnestly. "Let's not waste a lot of time on this one, please. Amen."

Beverly's head hurt. Boy did it hurt, and the noise was unbearable. She didn't know if she could handle it any longer. She would die if Terry didn't stop making all that racket. She would kill herself if she didn't die first. It was too much.

"What noise? All I'm doing is drying my hair. I made you some coffee."

"That's a good girl. Are the boys still asleep?"

"No, they're with Joe. He said you said it was okay," she shouted over the hum of the blow drier.

"Terry! Can't that wait?"

"Sure. Bad, huh, Bev?"

"The worst. I feel like I've been hit by a truck. Oops, bad simile. Ever been hung over, Terry?"

"I never get the chance," she mumbled as she went to get Bev a cup of coffee.

"Why?"

"Because I usually puke after my second drink. I've never kept enough down to get hung over. Steve is the one who ends up holding my head, so he cuts me off early. Nothing worse than a sick drunk. Maybe I'm allergic."

"Why didn't somebody cut me off... or at least shut me up?"

"Why? Did you step in it?"

"You wouldn't believe it."

"You remember everything?"

"Everything." Right down to Reverend Joe's britches. "I really made an ass of myself. Was Joe mad?"

"No. I'm surprised you even remember last night. You were really blasted."

"I'm sorry, Terry. About the crying and all. Booze does that to me. Makes me crazy and mouthy."

"And honest?"

"No, that was just the scotch. Things aren't all that bad. I'm doing real well, honey, honest. I had no business unloading on you. You have your own life to worry about. Don't worry about mine, okay?"

"You know what they say, Bev. Something about drunks and children never lying. You never mentioned Guy before."

"Uh-oh."

"You don't remember everything, do you?"

"Don't tell me. I don't even want to know. What did I say about Guy?"

"Well, make up your mind."

'Tell me. What did I say about Guy?"

"I think... everything. If there's anymore, I don't want to know about it."

Swell, Bev thought. A good little girl just learning about true love and honest sex and she briefed her on theories about sexual dysfunction and lousy lovers. What a nice big sister. "Well, I have no business giving you lectures on chastity anymore. Now you know."

"Beverly, I wasn't born yesterday. Do you really think I don't understand why you were sleeping with Guy? Why didn't you tell him he was a dud?"

"Because. He didn't want to know."

"As simple as that?"

"Yeah, sometimes it's just that simple. He wouldn't have heard me if I had told him. See, Bob was the kind of husband who wanted me to be happy and content in life, and in bed. So I wasn't prepared for someone like Guy. He didn't care about anyone but himself."

"How did you break it off with him?"

"We just sort of wore it out, Terry. There was no way to communicate being together, so we couldn't communicate parting. I decided to move back to Ohio. He said, 'Gee, I'm really going to miss you, baby. Maybe I'll get a flight up there sometime.' It was really very easy."

"That's too bad, Bev. I'm sorry that happened."

"Yes, well, it's over and done. And nothing for you to worry about. You just love Steve and chances are you'll have a long, happy life with him. No reason you shouldn't." Unless he just dies on you or something. "I'm fine. I'm hanging right in there."

"Sure."

"Are you going out tonight?"

"Do you need me here?"

"No."

"Well, then I'll cook dinner for Steve and help him with his laundry, which is our usual wild Saturday night. But I'll sleep here again if it's okay. I have my key."

"Is he picking you up?"

"He should be here now. I'd better get my hair dry."

"And I better hide. I don't want to scare him."

"Get off it, Beverly. You're beautiful even when you're hung over."

Beverly the beautiful. Except for the saggy boobs and stretched belly, and stretched something else.

Mark and Chuck had fun... but, of course, that was expected. And what did they think of Joe? He was a real dude. And why hadn't he come in? He didn't have time. He said see ya or something. Yes, something. Something like don't call me, I'll call you. They didn't want any lunch because they stopped at Dirty Girty's.

Dirty Girty's? Yeah, but they didn't eat in the bar part. And Chuck exploded the ketchup onto a plastic plant. Well, thanks Joe. And she would paint the backdrop anyway. And she'd curl up with a good book and go to bed early. And she'd have a shot of self-pity with her tuna casserole.

Beverly didn't care if it was Saturday night, and she didn't care if the monster movies were on, they would go to bed at a civilized hour because they had to go all the way to Grandma's church in the morning. So, at the very civilized hour of 9:30 Mark and Chuck went to bed with the TV on in their room. You're a real tough guy, Bev.

There was really nothing wrong with hot chocolate alone on a Saturday night, Bev told herself. Nothing at all. The sound of the television in the boys' bedroom was drowning out the dinner music on the stereo. Big shots. They'd never make it past the news to see the monster movies.

Since she had stopped having babies, she had stopped getting new bathrobes. She could have put on those lovely new lounging pajamas; an original somebody-or-other. They better be original; they were expensive enough. But lonely Saturday nights made you feel much sorrier for yourself if you had on the rattiest old robe you could find. And she did. And she was doing a real good job of feeling sorry for herself too.

It was not as though her marriage—all twelve years of it—had been perfect. It had been pretty typical. She fell in love, married. She worked for a while, which meant they fought about the chores. She got pregnant, which meant they fought about everything. Money, sex, time spent together, the smell of roses—everything.

She got pregnant again and they nearly split up; they had a seven-year itch; a real struggle. An enormous struggle. About the time Chuck came out of diapers, their marriage had settled into a comfortable habit. Blissful, amiable. She and Bob had finally become very good friends, co-conspirators.

Sometimes she didn't miss her husband as an individual as much as she missed her marriage. There had been someone to call in a crisis. Someone who fell asleep on the couch, someone who didn't dare mention her thighs unless he felt like discussing his paunch. Someone with whom to fight. Once they had really figured out how to fight, it had been a rare pleasure. Beverly didn't want to remarry and go through all the adjustments again; she wanted to wake up and find she had been married for a dozen years. When she thought of that it made her miss Bob so much. It was enough to make her weep.

Doorbell? At 10:10? What the—? He wouldn't. He did. It was the good preacher.

"What are you doing here?"

"We had a date. Remember?"

"But I thought... I don't know what I thought. Come in."

"You probably thought I had never seen anyone as stinking drunk as you were. And on five drinks. Is this how you dress for a date?"

"You don't like it? Never mind, I'll go crawl into something less comfortable. Give me a minute."

It was enough to make a person mad, Bev thought. Why was he coming around now? It would be different if they'd had a good time, but their evening together was a bomb. Didn't ministers go to bed at ten or something? She hadn't made coffee, of course, and she could hear the cupboard doors banging. She never kept neat cupboards. He was probably also immaculate. She was strictly a surface cleaner.

Since he was very nicely dressed and just coming from a fancy dinner party, Beverly begrudgingly pulled on a pair of jeans and a T-shirt. No bra. What good were secrets now? She was not very excited about this. Nosy preachers.

"You forgot the coffee," he said.

"I trust you found everything you need?"

"Had to really look. Why do you keep the coffee under the sink?"

"I don't know," she replied, completely exasperated.

"I hope the cups aren't in the garage."

"They're not!"

"What's the matter, Bev?"

"Nothing is the matter. What are you doing here? What is this?"

"This?"

"This! What do you want to hang around here for? Why are you bugging me? What do you want from me?"

"How about if we take one thing at a time. Why don't you want me around? Are you running away from me, or something else?"

"I'm not running away from you," she said indignantly. "Look, you're a nice guy. You can find a nice young virgin in your church who would be thrilled to have you pay attention to her. You don't have to hang around here and help me out. I don't need kindness and aid. You don't have any pastoral duty here."

"Great. I won't help you out. Now, can we just be friends?"

"Why do you want to be my friend? We're not even close to the same age."

"Come on—we're close. Within a decade at least, huh?"

"Look, I don't need anymore friends. Didn't you see enough last night to know we have nothing in common?"

"Give me a break, Beverly. I know you're not really a drunk. What are you afraid of? Go ahead, blast me. Tell me what's really on your mind."

"I'm not afraid of anything. I'm certainly not afraid of you!"

"Bull."

"Is that anyway for a minister to talk?"

"What do you care? Come on, let's have it."

"I don't want your preaching. I don't want to be saved and rescued. I don't want you to pull me out of my despair. I just want to be left alone."

"Okay, I won't preach and I won't rescue you."

"You'll try. Oh, you'll try. It couldn't be the scotch or the way I dressed that's got you turned on. You get your jollies from a lost soul, don't you? A poor sad little widow who needs your ministering. Go home. Just go."

"Is that what you think? That the only reason I'm here is because I think you need repentance and deliverance? Oh, you're dead wrong."

"Well then, what?"

"How about being attracted to a woman with a nice smile? How about liking you because you seem fun, even silly at times?

Or, because you're gutsy— you're making it in spite of a lot of problems—and that's appealing. And you have cute kids. But you're a regular snob."

"I am not a snob!"

"You are too! You don't want to go out with me because I'm a minister. That's a real snob." Two little heads peeped out from the hallway. Joe turned to the kids. "Ever see anybody have a good fight before?" They both nodded. "Then get out of here and let us fight."

"We're not fighting."

"Then what the hell are we doing?"

"Discussing this ridiculous situation."

"Very loudly. Very damn loudly!"

"It'll never work. We can't be friends. We're just too different."

"Why? Just tell me why."

"Because you're a nice Christian minister and I don't even believe in God."

"Why?"

"Why? Are you crazy? What kind of pervert are you? Can't you guess why? Do I have to draw you a picture?"

"Yes."

"Oh, God," she cried. He hadn't even really tried to reach her soul yet, and she was letting it bleed for him. Angrily, hatefully, with tears streaming down her cheeks and a pain in the pit of her stomach, she began to shout. "Where was God when that truck lost its brakes and smashed into Bob? Where was He when Bob was in pain, bleeding, dying, turning into a vegetable? God wasn't there when I begged for Bob's life, or for his death. End the pain, I prayed. And then I still prayed. Okay, you took him, God, so get me through this. But I'm not through it. I'm not even close. I have not one reason to believe. Not one."

"Okay," he said. "Pretty good reasoning. Come here."

Why was it whenever anybody said "come here" she did? She went right to him and slobbered all over his nice shirt. At least he helped her. He held her and let her cry. Ministers were trained to do that sort of thing. They probably had a course in comforting weeping women.

Almost two years and she was still crying. Sometimes she had a picture of herself as old and gray, an elderly grandmother still sniveling over her husband's death. It was over and done with and the tears still came. The well should be dry. And it was so ugly. This thing, this necessary release was so ugly. Tired. So tired. Sleep was the hard part. It wasn't easy to get used to sleeping in a king-size bed alone. And if you did get to sleep, sometimes you started seeing uniformed people and bright red bandages. What would ease the pain? A friend? Not so far.

So cry it all out, Beverly, Joe thought. No simple matter, this business of grief. He knew that as well as anyone. Two little heads peeped out around the corner. Sure, they had seen their mom cry plenty. Joe gave them the okay sign with his thumb and middle finger. Then he shook his fist at them and they disappeared again.

"Did you ever see anyone die, Joe?"

"Yes."

Sure he had. Ministers did that sort of thing too. They made hospital rounds just like the doctors. The doctor takes care of the body and the minister takes care of the soul.

"I mean someone you loved. Really loved."

"Yes."

"And you still believe in God?"

"Yes."

He would. "Well, that's why there's no point in our friendship. It's your whole career, and I can't even accept it as a hobby."

"Beverly, I didn't ask you to accept God. I asked you to accept me."

Dirty trick, Joe. "And you promise not to press the God thing?"

Joe lifted her chin with a finger. He was looking over the swollen red eyes. There, in his own deep blue eyes, was wisdom. Sincerity. But she would have to be blind not to see that he'd rather kiss than preach, even under the circumstances. When he spoke, his voice was soft. "The God thing, as you call it, is my life. First before you, first before all things. If you don't want to hear about it, I won't tell you. I won't try to change you or convince you. But that's as far as I go. I won't change myself."

"But you'll pray for me." It was more of an accusation than a question.

"I think you know the answer to that."

"Well, it'll never work. You'll get fed up with me in no time. It just can't work."

"Why don't we just get to know each other? You don't have to have any special kind of faith to get to know me. All you do is answer the door when I knock. Why don't we see what happens?"

She sighed. "I guess I just can't figure out why it's so important to you to get to know me."

"I can't figure out why you don't want me to."

"Well, shoot, I've been let down."

"Oh," he said. "And I suppose you're the only one?"

"Okay, okay. We'll be friends, you win. Nice, platonic friends. And you want to get to know me. So, what do you want to know first?"

"First—is it coffee yet?"

"I'll check. Second?"

"Second—do you like anything besides scotch? I'm not wild about scotch."

Five

B ev did like something other than scotch. It seemed Joe was not so turned off with brandy. Of course, it wasn't the taste of his mouth that concerned him because he only occasionally accepted the offered drink. It was the taste of her mouth. Well, what the hell, kissing was allowed in nice platonic relationships. Just a little though. Joe didn't like to kiss too much. He truly liked painting backdrops for the Sunday school program and taking the boys to the gym.

And Beverly truly enjoyed Joe. It was funny, because nothing would have pleased her more than to have not liked him, to be bored with him, or turned off by him. She found his control amazing. If she didn't suspect that he was turning blue praying for her in private, it would seem he didn't give a damn about her soul.

But he liked the way she looked in jeans. He said so more than once. "Some women just can't wear jeans the way they're meant to be worn. You can." That, she assumed, was how a minister told a woman she had a nice ass.

So they painted backdrops and went to the games Joe refereed. It happened that Carl Panstiel had a nine-year-old boy playing basketball and he and Bev crossed paths. Carl tried not to reveal that he was overjoyed to see Bev at the game, assuming she came because Joe had invited her. Bev guessed from the orgasmic expression on his face that Carl had played cupid from the start.

"You're a dog, Carl."

"Beverly, what a thing to say."

"You planned it. 'Help me with the Christmas program.' You dog."

"Bev, that's just not so. I'm simply glad to see you're going out with a nice guy like Joe."

Oh, brother. Well, at least he didn't ask if she had filled her prescriptions, which she hadn't. And he didn't offer to give her the name of a colleague who would be obliged to help her out since Carl knew the situation and the beau. Bev and the preacher were simply pals. Playing it straight. Nice and platonic. Ministers didn't get turned on.

But she said, "Thanks, Carl."

And he said, "You're welcome."

"See! You're a dog!"

"I'm a dog." And he was, he thought as he grinned, a mighty pleased dog.

There was comfort in routine. Bev saw Joe fairly often, but he wasn't pressing her. He helped with the painting once and then turned the youth group loose on her. He invited her to the games and the boys loved it. She made him dinner a few times and he took her out to dinner again, and this time she drank conservatively.

Terry stayed with Bev on the weekends. She would baby-sit if Bev was going out, and if Terry had a date with Steve, Bev's curfew was more lenient than was their parents'.

Terry and Bev had not always been close. At least not like Bev and John had always been. When Bev moved back to Ohio, she found Terry grown-up. She was the baby of the family. Now she was a woman.

In her second year at the university, Terry had to live at home because of expenses. She needed the babysitting money, and she also needed some time away from her parents. She was testing independence and finding it suitable. Terry was pretty, dependable, sensible. And Beverly actually admired her.

And Terry was on the pill.

Well, it was better than sleeping with Steve and using no birth control. Still, Bev was shocked and she couldn't quite hide her disappointment. It was a very old-fashioned idea, this notion Beverly had that a twenty-year-old woman should abstain until marriage. But with Terry it seemed so different. Terry had only just turned twenty and couldn't possibly be so sure about what she was doing.

"Did," Terry corrected.

"Well, it's not too late," Beverly the wise said.

"It is too, and you know it."

Yes, it definitely was, and she knew it. "But are you so sure this is the right guy? So sure you're going to be married?"

"Only as sure as I can be at my grossly immature age.

"Don't be flippant."

"Then don't act like Mother. Jeez."

"There's something to consider. What would Mother say?"

"I can only guess. Shall we try her?"

"Terry, you're being snotty."

"And you're being a hypocrite. You agree with me, you understand me, and you're too damned stubborn to admit it. You're being a big sister and not a friend. Why don't you level with me for once? You and Bob did the same thing."

"What?"

"Well...?"

"That's none of your business. Besides, you know all about my secret troubles. And I'm older than you. Wiser."

"Well, did you or didn't you?"

"Would you believe me if I said no?'

"No."

"Then I'll spare you. God, how you get under my skin with your almighty maturity. Who taught you so much about love and life in your whole twenty years?"

Terry shrugged. "Maybe I'm just self-motivated."

"Well, it's your life, so I won't try to change your mind. But don't come to me for a love nest away from home. Don't you dare use me."

"You know better than that."

She did know better than that, but it had to be said. Love is blind. It can also make a negligent baby-sitter.

"And you knew Steve and I were making love before I told you too. You know I love him and it is not casual. I know it would show to someone like you."

"Like me?"

"You're not in the dark, Bev. You're not fooled or foolish. I wanted to talk to you because I trust you. Didn't you really want to know?"

"I guess not."

"But why?"

Because now even Terry, little Terry, had someone. "Because it's not easy to face, honey. You've been the picture of purity in my mind. And love is not always blissful. Sometimes it hurts. Hurts so bad you think you will die. I don't think I wanted to believe you had reached that point."

"Sex with someone you love doesn't hurt, Bev. And it isn't dirty."

"No, honey, it's not. There is nothing nasty about what you and Steve have. And I hope it grows and gets more beautiful with the years. I just don't want you to ever get hurt. But that is my problem, not yours. I love you for wanting to be that honest with me."

"Beverly," she murmured, sniffing. "I'm so glad you came home."

"Me too, honey. Me too. Um... Terry?"

"Huh?"

"Do you think I'm... turning into our mother?"

Terry laughed and wiped her tears. "I think there's a good chance that you might."

"Sorry. I'm glad I'm home too."

Now, at least, she was. She had moved at the end of August because that was the best time of year for her. Bev had a passion for the fall, and some of that was because of the passion Bob had for her in the fall.

When they were young, both in college, they would go for long rides to see the hillsides come alive with color. She loved the scenery and she loved it better when they stopped the car and pulled out a blanket and did what Terry and Steve were doing without all the sophisticated protection. Well, what the hell, she'd loved him, hadn't she? And she married him, after all.

Bev, remarkably, enjoyed the fall even without Bob. She took the boys on a long ride to see the beauty. Forced them was more the word. It was not all she hoped for. It was a five-and six-year-old duet that moaned and groaned throughout the entire affair until she stopped the car and threatened to cram the picnic lunch down their throats if she heard one more gripe.

It wasn't easy to build an entire life around two little boys, even if they were your entire life. There had to be something more. So when she had settled herself in the Waspy section of the

Columbus suburb, she had set up her painting in the extra bedroom.

She knew she would never be a famous artist, and maybe she didn't want to be anymore. There was a time, when she was much younger, when an art teacher had said she showed such promise that Bev painted away her every moment with a vision, destiny calling her. Her vision turned into a degree in art education. She had taught ninth-grade art for three years after marrying Bob and hated every minute of it. Now she painted for pleasure, having learned that destiny can be a terrible liar.

She had begun to think that she could be content; the kids in school, her ridiculous part-time job, the beauty of the fall to inspire her painting, and a comfortable home. And then came winter. Cold and messy. She didn't get many calls for modeling and even the family gatherings she had dreaded were infrequent. She was downright depressed. Life was a pain in the neck. Bob had a nerve sneaking out and leaving her alone to raise her sons to be decent men. What kind of a guy would do that—promise to grow old with you and then split? A real louse, that's what kind.

When the last link was about to slip, Bev had reluctantly agreed to a relationship with Joe. It led to long discussions about popular issues and controversial subjects. She found out that adult companionship was something more. And to her amazement, she and Joe agreed on a great many things. They were just getting around to talking about sex and Bev was dying of curiosity. Getting a little excited, feverish, as a matter of fact.

"Why? Do you think ministers don't know about sex? You think ministers don't have some good questions about it? Certainly we're called into domestic situations that involve sex. God likes sex. He fixed it."

"Well, you're not counseling me; we're on a date. Hey, this is a date, no matter what you say. It seems like you're avoiding the subject with me."

Joe laughed. "You know something, Beverly? There's nothing wrong with me. I'm progressive. You're the one who's hung up."

"Well, what about sex before marriage?"

"What about it?"

"Do you think it's wrong?"

"I think it's a sin. Wrong."

"It's very popular."

"Why wouldn't it be? It feels good."

"How do you know?"

"I do a lot of reading."

"Don't you think maybe it's a good idea? I mean, it's a very important part of a marriage. I've been married, so I know more about this than you do. I think it should be checked out."

"That is a good reason, but it is still just an excuse not to make a commitment and not to practice restraint. Putting aside all the God stuff, as you call it, if you can choose someone with whom you are compatible in life, a person who is willing to work out all problems from money to sex, and who turns you on, you'll be fine. If both people love each other honestly, have faith and communicate, there is no reason to worry about how they'll get along in bed. They'll help each other in all things; they'll help each other sexually. I think that in sex as in the rest of life it is only give and take, compromise, tolerance, understanding, et cetera."

So who could argue that? "Is that what you tell the young people? To wait in good faith?"

"Yep. You think I should tell them to screw around and have a ball?"

"What about love?"

"Nice. What about it?"

"Doesn't that make it right?"

"Right? It makes it decent, I don't know about right."

"Well, jeez, everything must be a sin."

"Look, there are nice kids in my office who have screwed that one up, you should pardon the expression. They're good people and they're only human. God is understanding and willing to consider all sorts of extenuating circumstances. My job is getting people through stuff like this. I try to do my very best. I believe what I believe."

"Did you ever ask God if it was all right to make love to a woman even though you weren't married?"

"Yes."

"And what did He say?"

"He said no."

"And if you did it anyway, what do you think He'd say?"

"Something like, 'Shape up, Joseph.'"

"And what would you say?"

"I'd say,"—long silence—"please forgive me."

"You really mean that, don't you? You really mean that!"

"Oh, shit, you missed the whole point. First, I'd tell God how I feel about her, and I'd get advice from Scripture and the Horse's Mouth. And then if I still messed up, we'd work it out. There is nothing that can't be worked out. Beverly, you build altogether too many restrictions into this whole thing. You'd make a crummy God."

She giggled. "Joseph, did you say shit?"

"Accidentally. I accidentally said it, so I apologize."

"Well, now, see, that's what happens to young people. They start kissing, touching, falling in love, and they accidentally make love and—"

Joe was looking at her with a very superior smile, so she immediately stopped explaining it to him. "Nice try, Bev. I was a teenage boy once, and I can vouch for the fact that no sexual act of a teenage boy was ever an accident. It was carefully planned for years. The only thing he isn't sure about is the supporting cast. Don't you remember the rings all the guys used to have pressing through the leather of their wallets? Not that they had a clue how to put them on..."

"You're so sure about all of this," she said, amazed. "I wish I were that sure."

"You know my number."

"You'd love that, wouldn't you? You're all set to jump right in there and save my soul."

"Yep."

"Well, forget it."

Nope. "What are you doing for Christmas? Going to your folks?"

"Just for Christmas Eve. Are you going home?" Home for Joe was Los Angeles.

"No, I have lots to do. It's our busy season, you know. I was just wondering, do you give the kids money and let them shop?"

"Yes."

"Would you like me to take them to the mall? I know you could do it, but it might be kind of fun for you to be surprised with what they pick out for the grandparents and all that. I'd enjoy it."

"I think that would be very nice. Thanks."

Six

It wasn't easy to find John with time on his hands, but Terry was so insistent over the phone that he pushed aside his schedule and promised to meet her for lunch if she would come to the hospital cafeteria. He was late, which was usual for John, and Terry was already done eating when she saw him push his way through the line.

"This is nice. Do you bring all your dates here?"

"What dates?"

"Come on, John, I'm not that simple."

"I only date women with apartments who like to cook and do laundry. And other things. Now, what's the urgent family matter? Christmas present for Mom and Dad?"

"As usual, dear brother, we put in a crummy ten dollars for you, which you will never repay, and signed your name to the jackpot gift. The problem is Beverly."

"What's the matter with Beverly?"

"She's having a bad time, John. She doesn't have anyone for the boys. Mark said that when she gets a new boyfriend they glom onto the boys and once Bev's caught, they're ignored again. I figured it's kind of your place, you know?"

"Jeez. Yeah, my place. I barely have time enough to shower. I don't know how I can."

"Well, you better think about it. If you have a couple of hours, you better run out to Bev's and just hang around with the kids or something. You're just going to have to, John. They need a man who is closer to their father's age, someone permanent."

"She's not doing well? No fellas?"

"She's sort of dating Joe Clark. She says it's no big deal, that they're just friends. He's been horsing around with the boys a little, but what if they stop dating? Mark and Chuck keep losing

their main man over and over. Uncles don't usually desert like
that, get what I mean?"

"You're really serious. Tell me more."

"I don't know if I have the right. See, all I really know is what
Beverly spilled one night when she was drunk. It was not our
usual Beverly, but this completely broken-down, lonely, aching
little widow."

"Drunk? Our patron saint Beverly?" Beverly had a reputation
for being the responsible and controlled member of the family.
Mouthy, but controlled in her actions.

"On her first date with the preacher."

"Tacky. Very tacky."

"Agreed."

"Well, what did she say?"

"She had an affair after Bob died. The guy was a real jerk; he
even had her believing she had some kind of orgasm
impairment—she actually went to a doctor about it. Since then
she's been out with a guy who's gay, two married men, one single
sex maniac who nearly raped her when she wouldn't put out, and
now she's dating a preacher."

"Hmm. Beverly may be getting a little kinky."

"And they use her something awful, John. One jerk wanted a
woman to play house with, others need some sex, or—shoot,
maybe Beverly's right. Maybe Joe Clark is going to get his jollies
trying to save her soul. Come on, John. She's having lousy luck.
Help me help her."

Of course John would help. He loved Beverly. He just hadn't
known it was that bad. He wasn't exactly good with kids, but he
loved the boys too. After lunch he fished ten dollars out of his
pocket and promised to get over to Bev's within the week.

Terry pinched his cheek. "Guilt looks good on you, kiddo.
Thanks."

John started helping by dropping by and taking the boys to a
kiddie matinee and Beverly was surprised. He dropped by again
and took them sledding and she was amazed. Then he told her
straight out that he was going to do his best to see that they had
the companionship of a regular man forever, or until they had a
stepfather to do that. She threw her arms around him, kissed him,
and cried. Then she told him she loved him like a brother.

"I'm going to need love if I start spending my free time here. That nurse I've been dating isn't going to love it."

"Now, John, don't spend all your spare time here. You need a social life, too, and we understand that."

"Would it be a waste of time, Bev?"

"No. They need you."

"Doesn't the preacher play with them?"

"Terry! I should have known. Yes, he's terrific with them, but he'll be moving to his own church in the fall and then bon voyage. They need someone who's not going to leave them. I love you."

"I love them and you, too, honey. I've just been too busy to notice."

Things were looking up for Beverly after all, it seemed. Beverly had Joe, nice, platonic Joe, and John and Terry. Beverly was happy. She laughed. She didn't suffer from self-pity as much. Beverly, the lovely, busy, motherly, sexy, independent woman. Well, she could still have used a little romp in the sheets, but she couldn't have everything.

The Christmas pageant was a smash. The scenery was a godsend. The kids didn't louse up, the minister was a hit, the congregation was enchanted, Beverly was exhausted, and Joe Clark was falling in love.

Help me, Father, I'm so weak. What can I do to make her see, Lord? She won't come to me, Father. She won't let me through. I really love her. God, I love her all over. Oh, Father, I want her. She's afraid and alone. She thinks I want her soul. I want way more than that. Give me strength, Father. Give me a sign. Tell me when. Amen.

Christmas Eve was baked ham and relatives. Holidays were easier when there was family. And there was family. Was there ever. Great-grandparents, grandparents, aunts, uncles, cousins, and others. Joe was one of the others. Bev felt a little sorry for him. He wouldn't have all that family jazz for Christmas and he was just the type to go for it. So, Bev asked Delores if Joe would be welcome for Christmas Eve and Delores wanted to bake a wedding cake. She didn't say so, but Bev knew she was delighted.

Joe was Bev's tagalong for Christmas Eve. Mark and Chuck were more than thrilled to have him come. He told a Bible story to the children, and then the adults all went to the candlelight service at the church. Joe gave the sermon. The usual run-of-the-mill Christmas story.

But when Joe told the congregation about the birth of Christ, Bev really listened. Carefully. She tried to ignore the goose bumps it gave her and the excitement in her stomach. It was a very touching story whether you believed it or not, right? All this God business was a lot of nonsense. Go ahead, admit it, God. You're not really up there, are You? If You're really up there, say something. Say it loud. I'm a little hard of hearing.

A small voice in the back of her heart, or soul, or mind, said: I gave you life. I gave you family. I gave you Joe, your salvation. Don't get sore because I took Bob. I had my reasons.

She ignored it. Nonsense.

Beverly was glad she had decided to stay home on Christmas morning. She enjoyed watching the boys open their presents. She didn't want to yank them out of bed and drag them off to Grandma's house. It was like taking a tranquilizer because you thought you might be nervous later. Christmas morning should be spent in pajamas. It was. They tore into everything joyously. They loved all the presents. She was a terrific Santa Claus.

The boys hauled their booty off to their bedroom. They had reached an age when the bedroom held new importance. They were beginning to retreat to that sanctuary for private play. They played with new intensity now. It used to be the louder the better, and now it was the more real the better. They could pretend with flair and act out the parts dramatically, with Mark the producer and Chuck the stunt man.

So Beverly left them alone and started picking up the wrapping paper. That's when it hit her again. Daddy wouldn't see them. Daddy wouldn't be back. Did they miss Daddy as much as she did? Of course not. She wasn't even sure they remembered him; they'd been three and four when Bob died. Daddy was only a memory now, the perfect, superhuman man who used to be. But Bev remembered. All too well.

A tear traveled down the "merry widow's" face. It wasn't an angry or bitter tear. It wasn't a sore, or hurt, or pathetic tear. It was longing. Plain simple longing for the finest man, the finest love, the finest feeling she had ever had. There would never be another. She would never find it again. He was the best, the most wonderful, the grandest... God, how could any mortal be so perfect?

Well, there was no use pretending. He was. He loved her completely. Maybe not perfectly, always, but completely. He was thrilled with her when she bore their sons, no matter how rotten the pregnancy and night feedings were. He wanted to give her happiness and pleasure, ranging from multiple orgasms to a dishwasher if it made life better. He was clean and good. He was proud and committed. He must have been committed; he had stayed with her through the worst. They spoke already consummated vows in church and baptized their sons because they wanted to do everything right. He encouraged her in many things, and pulled her out of more than one depression. He had vitality. He worked hard, played hard, and loved hard. He had a lust for life... and now he was dead. Smashed and crushed in a horrible accident, and dead. Why had they not yet named a saint after him? Everyone liked Bob. Not least of all Bev.

That was the crux of it, of course. Bob had become her good friend. Her best friend actually since she was seventeen years old. Well, you have tiffs with best friends, right? Eventually, they could talk about everything from his feelings of inadequacy to hers. They had settled into a solid, satisfying marriage. It had become comfortable and unthreatening. And gone. Very horribly gone.

So here comes the anger again. Why? Why? Why? Not fair. Not fair at all. I needed you, you lousy bastard, and you ran out on me. I was good to you.

You said I wasn't bad as far as wives go. I cooked, the house was clean most of the time, and I did everything in bed you wanted to do. And I loved it. That's right, I loved it. No one has done that for me but you. I had your babies, ironed your shirts, and loved you... so much. What am I supposed to do now? What now? I still love you, damn you, and I'll never, never love that much again. How could I? Why should I? Oh, Bob, help me. I'm drowning again. Oh, God, help me. Are You there? Are You even there? I need something. Anything. Help. Oh, God, oh, God, oh, God.

The goddamn doorbell. On Christmas morning while I'm crying. The nerve. Probably the paperboy here for his present. Some people have some goddamn poor manners.

"Merry Christmas," Joe said.

"Merry Christmas yourself," she said with a sniff.

"What's the matter, honey? Lonesome Christmas?"

"It's nothing."

"Where are the boys?"

"Playing. I'll get them."

"No. Let them play." He had come in and was taking off his coat. He had presents. He was playing Santa. Beverly wasn't even dressed yet, but she had on those expensive lounging pajamas. She was beautiful even when she'd been crying over her dead husband. So kiss the tears away, stupid. What are you waiting for?

"Come here, baby."

Beverly the dependable. Well, what the hell, she needed a kiss. She needed a damn sight more than that, but not from a preacher on Christmas morning, thank you.

Joe held on. Her mouth tasted just as good in the morning as it did at night. She hadn't had a cigarette yet, which was a pleasant change of pace. She was beautiful in the morning. Visions of how she would look just waking up, naked between the sheets, a flush from their lovemaking still glowing on her cheeks...

"Reverend, please."

"Please what? I'll do anything you want."

"Remember your calling. Remember the commandments."

"Neither of us is married, Bev."

"There's something someplace about—"

Well, he certainly knew how to shut her up. He was on her mouth again, searching and begging. He was wonderful and strong. He was making her forget. He wanted her. Damn if he didn't really want her. It wasn't booze, sympathy, or anything false. She let the good preacher press her against the wall and she could feel the length of his handsome, strong body against hers. He was thirty and had never been married and she was thirty-four and had been married for twelve years and, when Bob had a reaction like that, she would follow into the bedroom and—

"Sorry, Bev. Got to have some coffee."

"Sorry?"

"Sorry I don't have any more control than that. Coffee. Please."

"There are times, Joe, when I think you're almost human."

"Don't remind me. God, don't remind me any more today."

"Are you praying, Joe, or taking the Lord's name—"

"I'm praying, for God's sake. Praying!"

Beverly hadn't seen a look of anguish quite that intense in a long time. Okay, you win. You're human. You have desires, too. Even ministers must have a limit. "Mark! Chuck! Joe is here!"

"Joe!"

They really loved Joe. Not just because of Bev, but because he had become their Joe. He was good for them. He was like a father at times. They respected and admired him. He brought them just what they wanted for Christmas. Mark had never mentioned a field hockey game to Bev, but he acted like it was a dream come true when it came from Joe. And Chuckie, naughty little Chuckie, loved the safe darts. And, of course, there was a children's Bible for each. Joe was hopeless.

There was a present under the tree for Joe too. They had decided together not to give it to him before Christmas because they didn't want him to feel obligated to reciprocate. It was a present from the boys to their good friend Joe, just because they liked him so much.

"I wonder what it is." He laughed as he tossed the basketball wrapped in bright foil paper up in the air.

"There's another one you can't guess," Mark announced.

He couldn't guess. It was in a box. He opened it like a kid on Christmas. He was happy, really happy. He pulled out the catcher's mitt and ball and his eyes lit up.

"Is this a hint?"

"Well, maybe when the snow melts," Mark said.

"We'll play catch, huh, Joe?" Chuck asked.

"Sure we will. Sure we will. Thanks, guys. Thanks a ton."

Beverly cried.

"Beverly, every time I see you you're either laughing or crying. When are you going to get your act together?"

"I'm sorry, Joe, it's just that... I don't know."

"I know, Bev. It turned out to be a decent Christmas anyway, huh?"

"I'm glad you stopped by."

Beverly hadn't made any big plans for Christmas. Just a quiet day for her and the boys. They wouldn't be impressed with a fancy meal, and in any case, she couldn't see slaving over a hot stove. She had been thinking in terms of tacos.

"Well, can I stay for Christmas dinner?"

It was a little embarrassing. She could pull a roast out of the freezer and stick it in the oven. It wouldn't be a complete disappointment.

"Of course, Joe. We weren't going to eat until much later though. Can you stay the whole day?"

He could. And cancel the roast. Joe had a turkey in the car. An already stuffed, premeditated turkey. And some refrigerated cranberry sauce and a bottle of red wine, which didn't go with poultry, but Joe didn't know anything about booze. It was the thought that counted.

"You're a turkey," was all that she could think of to say.

So Joe played with the boys and set the table and helped with the dishes and tucked in the cherubs, even though they were still going strong. Then he went back to where Bev was slumped. "I'm shot," she said, and moaned. "Worn out from basting that dumb turkey all day long. Why didn't you just ask if you could come over on Christmas Day?"

"Because you might have said no."

"Then that would have meant I didn't want any company."

"You would have thought that and you would have been wrong."

"You're a know-it-all."

"Thanks for the presents, Bev. It really means a lot."

"It was their idea, but you're welcome."

"That means even more."

"Come on, tell the truth. It's not me you want, it's them."

"It's all of you."

"Liar."

"It's not nice to call a minister a liar. It might even be a mortal sin or something. You're going to have to watch that sort of thing."

"I don't believe in mortal sins or ministers, remember?"

"Shucks, I forgot. Well, why don't you thank God for a good celebration anyway, just in case I'm right and you're wrong."

"Maybe later. Want some more wine, Joe?"

"Coffee."

"What's in coffee that makes you so dependent? Saltpeter?"

"Beverly, for God's sake, don't shame me. I have weaknesses like everyone else."

"I was thinking it was one of your strengths." She shrugged. She went to get him more coffee. She had coffee, too, instead of wine. Ministers had this way of turning people into puritans just by hanging around.

"If you can come here and sit beside me and behave yourself, I have something for you."

"Behave myself? Why, Reverend, have I been out of line?"

"Be serious. Come here." More kissing and hugging she suspected, which was as far as it went with good old platonic Joe. But it was something special, wrapped, and in a box. A present. A gold chain. Real gold. Real expensive too.

"You shouldn't have done this, Joe. I can't accept it. I'm sorry, I just can't."

"What do you mean, you can't. You can and you will."

"But I have nothing for you. I know you don't have a lot of money, Joe. Oh, it's beautiful. I'm sorry, I couldn't. Lovely, but I just wouldn't feel right. So pretty, but I can't." But it was going around her neck and she loved it.

"You really do like it, don't you, Beverly?" He was smiling that smile again. That sexy, glorious, divine smile. It was enough to give a woman cramps.

"You shouldn't have. Why?"

"Because I love you."

"You're crazy."

"Crazy in love."

"That's not a good idea, Joe. It wouldn't be wise to love me. Not healthy. Take back the chain, Joe. Please."

"Why?"

"Because I don't want tokens of love from you. Not until I can return them."

"It's a Christmas present, Beverly. Now, stop being juvenile."

Beverly was pretty easy, especially when it came to lovely little gifts. She would take the chain because it really seemed to give him pleasure and she would be polite, but she would not say "I love you too" because she wouldn't mean it.

But she would try out this love thing for a while. She wouldn't make Joe stop loving her, because it made her feel good. And she knew Joe wasn't a liar. If he said it, he meant it.

As if being pushed by some outside force, Joe was kissing her again. Well, after you tell someone you love them, it's only natural to kiss them. So he kissed her. And kissed her. And it happened again, for the second time that day. And it was getting to be embarrassing.

Beverly didn't mind. It was becoming more real to her. Joe was becoming more real. It had been only a month since they had met and she hadn't been able to dodge him yet. He was always there when she needed him. He comforted, coddled, pulled her through, and was starting to reach down inside of her and pull her out of herself. In fact, every time she uttered that tired old prayer out of sheer desperation, the doorbell rang. Coincidence, that's all.

Beverly was wickedly human. She encouraged him. She let him push her down onto the sofa with his body and led him. He was losing the battle. He was hungry and wanting, even more than she. She wanted him to lose this battle, admit defeat, succumb to the flesh. Hers. The sooner the better.

"Oh, God. Oh, God."

"No, Joe. It's Beverly. Beverly!"

No it's God I need now. Hurry! Faster, Lord, faster. Do something quick. Lightning. Hit me with Your best bolt. Oh, God, I could come alive in her. I know what's there. I've got a breast in my hand, an urge in my groin, and I'm slipping... fast. Please? Oh, please, just this once? I'm begging now, really begging."

"Let's go to the bedroom, Joe."

She couldn't really be saying that. She wouldn't just say that. I imagined it, right? I better check to be sure she didn't just say that.

"Bev, I want you, baby. I really want you."

"I want you too, Joe. But I can't."

"You can't?"

"I want to, but I can't."

"Well, why the hell not?"

"Because Mark and Chuck are giggling. We're caught."

"Shit."

"Joseph Clark!"

Joe jumped off the widow and the couch and headed out the door. Out into the cold dark night. Well, did she invite you to her bed or not? You were so damn busy praying, you couldn't even hear her. She was telling you to back off.

"What are you doing out there?"

"I'm stuffing snow in my pants. Get lost."

"Are you coming back inside?"

"Later. Put on some coffee."

Seven

Beverly was obliged to spend New Year's Eve alone. Joe was having a church party for all the young people who wanted to bring in the New Year with a prayer. She wasn't that far gone. She would stay home and nurse a scotch on the rocks.

Mark and Chuck were determined this year to make it to midnight or bust. They busted at about 10:30. Big tough guys. Bev was just getting around to fixing her scotch. Joe called.

He just wanted to say hello and wish her a happy New Year's Eve. He wished she would have come with him; she couldn't possibly be having any fun at home alone. She insisted she was having a fine time. He promised to call later to wish her a Happy New Year. That was fine, she told him, but she might go to bed.

At 11:00 she was wishing she had gone with Joe. She was bored. Scotch was not nearly as much fun as Joe. At 11:30 she was starting to drift off and decided to give up and go to bed. She wasn't having any fun. She had seen that stupid ball go down the pole at least a dozen times over the years. But before she went to bed she would have to answer the phone.

"Hi, baby. Happy New Year."

"Who is this?"

"Bob. Bob Stanly."

"Oh." Swell. Good old sex maniac Bob. He was a little drunk too. "Happy New Year, Bob. What are you doing in Columbus?"

"I'm here 'cause I know this great chick in Murphy. I wanna make up, sweetheart. I'm sorry, okay?"

"Okay."

"So can I come over for a drink?"

"Sounds like you've had enough to drink."

"Still the same old ice-cold bitch huh, Beverly?"

"Good-bye, Bob."

Nice guy. Picking on lonely widows on New Year's Eve. What a creep. And besides being a creep and a widow molester, he was going to drive her crazy all night by calling.

"Hello."

"I'm coming out, Beverly. I'm gonna teach you a lesson; warm you up a little."

"I'll call the police."

"Good. Maybe me and the cops will all have a turn on you. See ya, baby."

Now what? So call the police.

Nothing could wake Beverly up like an obscene phone call. She dialed the number of the police and talked to the desk sergeant for a little while. The police were not very upset about her little phone call. The guy was obviously drunk and wanted to stir up trouble. They would send a patrol car by when they could, but she shouldn't worry. It was a busy night. Lots of calls. She said, "Swell, but hurry anyway." The "merry widow" was spooked.

The minute she put the receiver down the phone was ringing again. Don't answer it, Bev. It's not midnight yet, so it's just that Bob Stanly creep. Let it ring. It's only twenty minutes to twelve.

That pervert was going to call all night, every three minutes, until she answered the phone. Nope, he was giving up. Which meant he wasn't calling; he was driving. Well, it would take him at least a half hour to drive to Murphy. If he were really coming.

Beverly couldn't believe that all over the United States people just like her were sitting home watching a ball go down a pole. So Happy New Year already. No cops yet. Busy night, y'know. As soon as they could, they would.

It was at times like these that Beverly was unable to conquer complete independence. She wanted to have a man sleep on the couch from about midnight until six A.M. just to keep the ax murderers away. She was afraid of people like Bob Stanly; men who came on like adjusted, healthy specimens with even a dash of sensitivity to add to it all. Was it the decent man next door, the cub scout leader, or church deacon who suddenly snapped and went crazy? What would have happened if she'd obliged him that night? Was this anger and frustration, or would he have found a way to frighten and abuse her even if she had complied?

She planned the escape routes, thought of possible weapons, and turned off all but one light. The neighborhood was quiet. The other half of her duplex had been empty for months. People didn't move at Christmastime. She peeked out the window and this time her heart nearly stopped. There was a car out there. A car she didn't know. She shook all over. She would be murdered if she didn't die of fright first. She would call the police again if she could only stop shaking.

"They're not there yet? I'll radio them again."

"Now, look, the guy is sitting in the car in front of my house, Sergeant. You're going to have to hurry. He's some kind of pervert. Come on, I'm scared."

"Lock the doors, Mrs. Simpson. Lock the doors and don't panic."

"The goddamn doors are locked, you simpleton. You think I was waiting for this cretin with them standing wide open? Now, get off your ass and get a cop out here before he chops me up in little pieces and flushes me down the toilet. And hurry!"

Oh, God, he was pounding at the door. It was definitely that Bob Stanly creep, calling her name, slurry drunken speech and all. "Come on, baby. Let me in. I ain't got all night, sweetheart. Let's have a little toss and then I can get back to the party."

Beverly crept closer to the door. She wanted the police to drag this maniac away. She was altogether too scared to look out the window. What if he had a gun? What if he shot the cops and then broke in? Should she wake up the kids or hope they would sleep through it? Wake them up so they wouldn't find her body in the morning. Let them sleep so that the pervert couldn't even know they were there. She'd have to be very quiet while he was killing her so she didn't wake up the—

"Come on, buddy, let's go."

Cops.

"Who're you? Get out of here, pal. I got some business with the lady."

Not cops.

"Get away from that door, friend, and I don't want any trouble."

Joe. Joe?

"Get lost, fella, and I mean it."

"I said, get away from that door. And I mean it."

"Oh, you mean it, do you? Well, we'll see."

Beverly shot to the door and looked out. Bob Stanly was even more drunk than she imagined. How he got to Murphy in one piece was the first miracle, and how he was still standing was the second. He wound up and took a big swing at Joe. The preacher stepped aside and Bob Stanly fell flat on his face in the snow. Beverly could have done that much. He couldn't have raped her with the help of five assistants. She opened the door.

"You okay, Bev?"

"Okay," she cried. "I'm okay, Joe."

Then the cops came. It figures. They took away the pitiful drunk and Joe got to overhear the little story about Bob Stanly. The police would call her in the morning about pressing charges and when they left she fell into the assistant minister's arms. Joe was really good at that sort of thing. He was ad-libbing along with the brow-stroking and forehead-kissing.

"Why did you come?"

"You didn't answer the phone."

"You weren't going to call until midnight."

"I wasn't going to call until after midnight. We were going into the chapel for worship and I decided to give you a call first. No answer."

"As simple as that," she murmured. A Divine power? Could no answer be an answer? "No answer." The story of my life.

"Well, I had a funny feeling. I just don't like you living alone. I think we ought to get married, Bev."

"I don't want to get married."

"Okay."

"Just okay?"

"I didn't think you were ready for that. But I don't like you out here alone. And I love you, remember?"

"I know. I'm afraid I just can't figure out why."

"Get serious."

"I mean it. I can think of about a hundred good reasons why you shouldn't."

"Like what? Never mind—there's maybe one."

"One? Which one?"

"You tend to be a lot of trouble. You get a little... you know, bossy."

"Oh, swell."

"But I guess I like that too."

"You must have a screw loose. Are you some kind of masochist? Why put yourself through this anyway? I really can't figure you out."

"Don't you know why I love you? Really? Come on, your ego is pretty damn healthy. Well, it's like this. The obvious, first. You have this terrific figure, which sort of got my attention. Then, there's this kind of smell—wrong word; there's something in your skin that appeals to me."

She was looking at him with a slight frown.

"Okay, that's the physical," he said, putting an arm around her. "There seems to be a lot to you, you know? It's like this—no matter what you feel inside, you feel it all over your whole body. When you cry, you cry from your toes. When you laugh, you laugh like a shooting star; there are these sparks and glitters everywhere. When you decide to tease, you're a riot. And when you get mad, you don't sulk or pout or snivel; you get really mad. A little too mad, maybe, but I like it."

"You're nuts. Whoever heard of someone falling in love because they like to be with a bossy person or liking the way someone gets mad. Jeez."

"A guy just can't be ordinary with you, Beverly. You challenge damn near every feeling that ever existed and a guy is forced to be everything he can be, or he just can't be with you. It's really neat. Besides, you make me laugh."

"Great. I'm a wit."

He laughed. "Yeah, and you might think that's no big deal, but it's a basic requirement. I happen to like to laugh. Keeps me, you know, happy." He kissed her cheek. "I really do love you, Beverly. I've been out with a lot of really nice women, but you're more. I've never felt it before. I never know if we're going to argue, make out, giggle, or have a good cry; you're unpredictable. At least there's something to you. Have you ever been out with a guy that, you know, has a lot going for him—good-looking, amusing from time to time—but you just can't get too excited?" She grinned at him. "See?" he shouted. He pointed a finger right at her face, smiling. "See? That's it—there's no slack. I like that. Come here."

"Wait a minute. Want some coffee?"

"No."

"You aren't planning to leave, are you?"

"Do you want me to stay?"

"Would you? Just tonight? I'm still a little shaky."

"Sure. Got a pillow and blanket?"

"Sure. Are you tired?"

"Nope. Are you?"

"Nope," she said, imitating him.

"So what do you want to do?"

"I want to talk."

"About what?"

"Your God trip."

"No kidding? I don't believe it."

"Don't get excited. I just want to talk, not get baptized."

First she wanted to know how Joe got so interested in God. Why, really why?

"It's not very exciting, actually. I was raised with the faith. Back when kids went to confirmation classes because their parents made them, I really got excited about it all. I kept it up through high school, when I was really square, and just like everyone expected, I went into the seminary as soon as I could."

"Just like that? No doubts?"

"Boy, did I doubt. But later, I had a battle with the Lord to end all battles. I accused Him, cursed Him, and then I ignored Him."

What brought all that on, it seems, was a little sister who had also found the Lord, or a reasonable facsimile. It made Joe question Him. May was a cute kid, a lovely child. She joined a cult of some kind and left home when Joe was in the seminary. She wouldn't correspond with her parents or Joe.

"We listed her as missing, but she was a runaway and we knew it. We knew about the crowd she was running with. My parents forbade her to see them and so she ran off with them. She was only sixteen.

"I found out just how many different cults there are; it's amazing. May's crowd was collecting money from Scripture readings and using some pretty heavy drugs to get spiritually closer. They set up and robbed a lot of people. They may have even murdered for all I know.

"I left the seminary to find her. It took me a year and I held her captive in a little apartment in L.A., trying to get her off drugs and deprogram her. But I failed. Flopped. I was no match for the drugs and delusions. She hit me over the head and ran off with the freaks. They took her out of the city, out of my reach. When I found her again, she was in a San Diego hospital, in a coma."

"Poor Joe."

"Poor May. She didn't make it. I don't think she suffered. How do you know if someone is suffering in a coma? I suffered. My parents suffered. I prayed and prayed, offered to trade every mortal gift I had for her life. For another chance. My answer came from a young intern who said, 'It's over, Joe. She's brain dead.' And we unplugged her and let her go."

"It wasn't easy on you, was it, Joe? Even with God?"

"How could He do that to me? I asked over and over. After I had given Him my life, He had taken hers. I begged Him to release her from death, to give us all another chance. I challenged Him with the grandest of miracles, and when He didn't perform, I called Him a liar; a welcher. I still can't believe that was me. I finally decided I wanted nothing to do with Him. Everyone else seemed to know May couldn't come back and that God wouldn't deliver on ultimatums. But I was going to really make Him prove Himself. I told Him I'd go to hell before I'd put up with any more bad deals. But I just went into the army."

"Was it pretty close to hell?"

"For me it was. I worked in a hospital. I saw a lot more sin and pain, even a little more dying. I had my own little fling with sin, and most of the time it didn't feel too bad."

"So, when did you go back to God?"

"I'm not exactly sure. I suffered more while I was fighting with Him than I ever had before, so I finally threw up my hands and said You win. I give up."

"And that was that?"

"That was definitely not that. Then I had to go through this incredible, laughable journey. I decided it wasn't enough to practice my faith in middle-class communities full of hypocritical Christians. It wasn't enough to teach Sunday school to spoiled little rich kids, play basketball, or read Scripture to a bunch of fat, lazy people who nodded off. They all just went home and sinned like crazy anyway. So I went May's route. I went into the inner city to drag doped-up kids to the Lord like human sacrifices. I had to save the lost causes, deprogram the confused youth, cure every drunk, restore hymens in the prostitutes. I worked in halfway houses, Salvation Army centers, and other less plush but necessary places. I was singing praises so loudly that I couldn't even hear God. My parents thought they had lost another child."

"So what was He saying while you were singing?"

Joe smiled. Beverly was listening so closely, like a kid hearing a bedtime story. She would never admit that she really wanted to know, that she herself was searching. She was afraid of the answer, afraid she might have to change. So relax, Bev. It's all right. It doesn't hurt. It feels good.

"He was trying to tell me that He needs people everywhere; that some are supposed to do the rough work with the lost souls in the slums and some are supposed to go to the suburbs and play basketball with the kids. A problem is a problem is a problem. A sin is a sin. They are not ranked in the order of their importance. Everyone needs love, attention, and guidance. Someone stands on a street corner, someone else in a pulpit. He said, 'Slow down, Joe. I didn't create you to save the world. Just the ones I send you. Go back to school. I'll let you know. I have other plans... for Christ's sake.'"

How could he say something like that, Bev wondered; something that could have sounded like some really good swearing and have it end up a prayer? Uncanny. Well, it was a very touching story. He should write a book or something. So how did the voice of God sound, exactly? Deep and gruff? Nice and calm? Joe was living in some kind of spiritual fantasyland, adding up coincidence and conscience to sound like the voice of God. Certainly unrealistic. Maybe even a little crazy.

"It's all very dramatic, but after all, it's just the story of one man's life. Lots of people are survivors. So you hurdled the bumps and claim your hero to be God. What do you expect me to get out of that?"

"Beverly, you asked. Didn't you really want to know?"

"Sure, and I appreciate the honesty. Now, what do you expect me to get out of that? Do you think that your experiences will convince me? Tell the truth now. Do you?"

Joe was sitting beside her on the couch, one arm resting around her and a foot up on the coffee table. He kissed her mouth, a warm and sensual kiss. "Scotch."

"I didn't think I would see you," she murmured apologetically.

"That's okay. Come here."

"Joe," she said, stopping him. "Did you ask God if it was all right to love me?"

"Nope."

"Why not?"

"I didn't have time."

"Well, maybe you should ask Him now. He might say no."

"Too late. Come here."

"I wanna talk."

"Okay, okay, now what?"

"Sex."

"Oh, Beverly, you wear me out. What about it?"

"Are we going to try it?"

"I hope so. I really hope so."

"After marriage?"

"I hope so. God, I hope so."

"Quit praying. Have you ever made love to a woman?"

"Yes."

"Who?"

"Beverly, ease up. It doesn't really matter who, now, does it?"

"Okay, were you in love with her?"

"Them."

"What?"

"The question should be 'them' not 'her.' And once I thought I was in love. Really had it bad. I didn't make love to her. I made love to other women that I didn't care anything about. And it felt pretty good."

"On your sin trip?"

"Yep."

"Were you ashamed and sorry?"

"Yes. Later though. Much later."

"What happened to the girl you loved?"

"She's married and happy. I don't love her anymore, Beverly. I love you."

"Did it just evaporate, that love?"

"No, honey. I threw it away. The sin trip, remember?"

"Joe, what am I supposed to do now? I know you really believe hard. You're so sure and unthreatened. I don't know what to do. I don't want you to save my soul. I want to be left alone. I don't want trials or commitments or any of that crap. I just want a scotch on the rocks, a nice man like you to love me, and a regular life. Do you understand?"

"Perfectly."

"So, what do I do now?"

"Why don't you just relax and enjoy it. Sounds like a good life."

"And what about God?"

"Well, you could ask Him, and I think he would say you're more acceptable to Him than He is to you. But if you really want to check all this out, you can pray, you can read the Bible, you can ask questions. You can talk to me. I won't hurt you. I love you."

"I know, you said that already. You want to trap me, rush me. God wants to trap me; that's why He keeps putting you on my doorstep."

"You talk as though He really exists, Bev. You're going to have to watch that sort of thing."

Joe was laughing at her. He thought the almighty confusion she suffered was real damn funny. But he stopped laughing and started kissing again. He was getting pretty good at it too. He was starting to touch again. Beverly was hoping he wouldn't stop touching. Oh, she needed him so badly. Maybe she ought to go ahead and have that IUD reinserted. Or fill those prescriptions. What about right now? It sure wouldn't hurt. It was so late at night and the boys were asleep and Joe was having that little problem again. She let him push her down and clung to him feverishly. She moved her hips under him. She loved it. He loved it. They both needed it.

"Oh, Joe...Joe!"

"I know. Baby, I know."

"But I don't want to get married."

"I know. It's okay."

"So what should we do?"

"We've got to do something. Fast."

"In the bedroom."

"Will the shower wake the boys?"

"You can shower afterward."

"No, I have to shower now. Right now."

Joe bounded off the couch and was heading for the bathroom. Beverly was stunned. Stunned and aching. "Joe! Come back here!"

"Go to bed, Bev. Now."

"Aren't you going to finish what you started?"

"Not tonight. Later, maybe."

Beverly simmered. Pretty soon she could hear the shower running. She squirmed more. It stopped. He might be all cooled off, but she was mad as hell. Damn all the self-righteous preachers. Who did this one think he was anyway? What was the great plan here? Get married and find out it was a mistake? No way. Over my dead body, Preach. I've been there, baby. I know what it's like to have it great and I know what it's like to have it lousy, which is the same as not having it, period. God, or no God, it was a basic human need, like eating, and she told him so the minute he came back into the living room.

"I agree." He laughed. "But I don't steal groceries either."

"Steal?" she asked him. "Why would you be stealing it? I'm offering it!"

"I know. What are you offering me, exactly, though? Sex? What makes you think that's all I need?"

"Oh!" The nerve. Making her look like the devil facing off with an archangel. She was ready to really have it out with him, but for some reason her anger turned into guilt. She tried to stay mad, but she felt guiltier. So she cried.

Two arms came around her and there was a rather familiar shoulder sopping up the tears. "It's okay, sweetheart. I know it hurts. It hurts me too. It's a very natural thing to want. But it's going to be all right, honey. I love you. You go to bed, get some rest. I'll be here in the morning."

And he was. Good old dependable Joe.

Eight

*I*n January Beverly started going to Maple Hills Christian Church regularly, right down to enrolling the boys in Sunday school. She enjoyed listening to Joe. Joe had a good pulpit voice.

In February John and Joe both took the boys to the gym three times. Joe was already there when John came for them, so they made it a foursome. Then Bev and Joe double-dated with John and the nurse he was seeing. Bev suspected that John liked Joe more than he liked his own sister. They were becoming close friends. Chums, in fact.

One Saturday afternoon when Joe brought the boys home he hung around and had a cup of coffee. He stood in front of the patio window and watched Mark and Chuck as they made a fort out of snow. Softly, to his back, Bev said, "I love you, Joe."

Something like a rocket hit Joe. He turned and looked at her. She met his eyes for a second and then turned around and walked back into the kitchen. When a guy has been waiting for months to hear those words and then she just turns around and walks away, what are you supposed to do? Follow her into the kitchen, or just apologize and go home?

"That's wonderful, Bev, but you don't sound particularly happy about it."

"I thought you should know."

"Well, thanks.... I guess."

"I didn't want to be in love with anyone, Joe."

"Well, those things happen. Should I apologize?"

"I'm not ready for it. This is going to take some time."

"You afraid?"

"Sure."

That should be obvious. When you're talking to someone about love and just keep on chopping carrots instead of kissing him or even looking at him, he should know you're scared to death.

"I won't hurt you, Bev."

"Not on purpose." It sounded like an accusation. He turned her around. He made her look at him.

"Bev, death hurts. Love doesn't. Try to relax."

"I'm trying."

"Feel it out, honey. Take your time. If you just let yourself, you'll feel good. And I'll be right here, ready to feel good with you."

"There's something I want to tell you about this and you're going to have to take it like a grown-up, all right?"

"Shoot."

"One of the reasons—part of the reason I love you—is, I mean, you are terrific, the most terrific man in the world, probably, but I can't stop myself from being in love with you because of the way you feel about me. I mean, you feel about me the way..." She turned away from him briefly, but he wasn't having that. He made her face him. Her eyes were a little moist, but she wasn't going to cry.

"Say it. It's all right."

"You feel about me the way Bob finally did. I think, anyway. There are a lot of things about me that other men wouldn't put up with."

"Because they're wimps."

"And you're not a wimp, huh? You think you're going to get through this in one piece? I am not convinced that I'm the best thing that could have happened to you."

"That's not really for you to question, now, is it?"

"I would really hate to be the one to—"

"Got some more advice for me, Mom?"

"Hey, come on, I'm thinking only of you."

"One minute you make me promise to be a grownup, the next minute you're trying to take care of me. Get it together, Beverly. Now, do you love me or not?"

"Yes. I love you."

"Then kiss me. Hard."

March came and there was a blizzard. Chuck got strep throat and Joe stayed the night because Bev was worried about the high fever. Bev had a fever too. The other kind. Joe had another shower. Beverly had strep throat. If she weren't so sick, Joe would have laughed. Beverly the temptress... with the real McCoy, strep. But because she was so sick, Joe called the doctor.

The doctor that Joe called wouldn't come out to the house, and he wanted Bev to go to the emergency room. Then Joe called John, but John couldn't leave the hospital. So, Joe called Carl, the friendly neighborhood ob-gyn. Carl would come out to the house. Carl wouldn't miss it for the world. He would come out and give Bev a shot and she could see John later for a throat culture.

Carl was thrilled to see that it was Joe who was nursing Beverly. Very thrilled.

"Stop smiling, Carl. I'm dying."

"You're not dying. Open up. Wider."

"What do you see?"

"Not what I'm used to seeing. I much prefer the other end."

"Carl, don't be a smart-ass. I'm dying."

"Okay, so turn up the other end and I'll save your life. This is a big dose, Bev. You're going to have to stay in bed for a couple of days. What's Joe doing here?"

"Probably praying... again."

"Maybe he ought to call your mother or Terry. You're going to need some help around here."

"Isn't this contagious?"

"Yes, have you infected Joe yet?"

"I tried. Boy, did I try. He's too pure to get strep throat."

"Well, he ought to have a throat culture anyway, just in case you sullied his purity."

"Oh, shut up, Carl."

"Okay, okay, just stay in bed. Alone."

"Get out of here, you monster."

Shortly after the blizzard, when Beverly's strep throat was all gone and the streets were getting sloppy again, Joe was trying very hard to catch up on his paperwork. People did not realize how much paperwork was involved in being a preacher. He was a little irritated when the phone rang because it rang often. Someone always had a problem, and half the time they were little, minor, irritating problems.

"Hi, Joe, it's Bev."

"Yeah, honey. What?"

"You must be in the middle of something."

"Sorry—no. Well, yes, but it's only paperwork, enough paperwork to sink the Titanic. I don't mean to sound impatient."

"You're not in a meeting or anything?"

"Nope. All alone. Why? You want me to talk dirty or something?"

"I'm at the hospital, Joe. My dad had a heart attack. Will you come?"

"Sure. Right away. Where?"

"County General. Fifth floor ICU. And Joe? I don't think it's too bad, but Mother's a little rattled, though John is here already, and I had to bring the boys with me. Please go ahead and pray all you want on the way over."

"Are you all right?" he asked.

"Sure. But this is a little scary. Charlie's only fifty-nine. He has a birthday coming up, but he's only fifty-nine."

He asked himself all the way to the hospital which voice she'd been using—her strong voice, her terrified voice, her pitiful voice, or her bossy voice. He couldn't quite remember. Joe was really worried about Charlie, but he couldn't help but wonder how this whole ordeal was going to affect Bev.

The ICU is an interesting place. Joe remembered May's ICU. There is a large care center full of white-uniformed people that is cordoned off like an experimental laboratory, outside of which there is a waiting room with furniture comfortable to sleep on, since quite a few people sleep there. They don't let you hang around in ICU, not ever. You get to sneak in about once an hour, take a look at this fully tubed person who doesn't seem to have any life left in them at all, then you have to quickly return to the little fake living room and sit, watching each person that goes in and out, wondering if they're doing anything to your person.

Beside the waiting room, there is always another room. In every hospital, everywhere. In that other room, which is like an office, with a desk, some chairs, and a phone, they talk to you. First to tell you how it stands, next to tell you what they're going to do, sometimes to tell you it's over.

Charlie Clinton's clan was gathered in the waiting room. Delores was twisting a handkerchief. Terry had a look of

unbelievable terror widening her pretty eyes, Mark and Chuck
were abnormally quiet and still, each holding a can of soda, only
Chuck's feet swinging a little. Very little.

"Oh, Joe," Delores said, rising and filling his embrace as
naturally as Beverly would. She began to weep instantly. He
looked over her shoulder toward Terry. Terry was immobilized.

"Have you been in to see him?" Joe asked.

"Yes." She wept harder. "Oh, he looks so terrible. Oh, Joe.
What am I going to do?"

"What did the doctor say?"

"They don't know the extent of the damage yet. He was at
work. That work is too hard. He's a foreman, but he gets right in
there with the men and works the drill press and the—"

"Okay, Delores, don't jump the gun here. Where's Bev?"

"Oh, she went to get something for—"

At that very moment Bev came around the corner with wings
on her feet. She was carrying a small basin and a glass of
something. She said a quick "Hi-Joe-thanks-for-coming" on her
way toward Terry. She knelt before Terry. Terry leaned her head
forward, over the basin, and with one hand Beverly pushed the
hair back from her face, wrapping it around Terry's ear so it
wouldn't canopy the basin, and with another hand she reached
over and squeezed Mark's knee. Joe was transfixed by her
caretaking.

On her way over toward Joe and Delores, she stopped and
whispered to Chuck, tousled his hair, and pulled something out of
her pocket. "These are smelling salts, Mother. Now, you come
and sit down and hold on to these. If you start to feel faint again,
put your head down, and if that doesn't work, break one of these
open, like this. Come on."

She took her mother over to a chair, beside Terry, and sat her
down. Then she went back to Joe.

"Terry's nauseated. Mother's faint. John is in there with the
cardiologist. Dad wanted you to come; he asked for you
specifically. I'll go in there with you."

"How are you holding up?"

"Me? Fine. Do you know that Terry has never been in a
hospital before? Never? Kind of unbelievable, isn't it?"

"Does anyone know how bad it is?"

"I think it's going to be all right, Joe. He didn't lose consciousness. Isn't that a good sign?"

"I don't know—is it?"

The big swinging doors to the intensive care unit slowly opened and John came out with the doctor. They were still chatting quietly. Part of what was so unnerving about these places was the quiet, intense way everyone talked.

"It's going to be all right," John said. "There doesn't appear to be too much damage. He's been sedated and there will have to be more tests, but so far I think we're in good shape."

"Thank God. John, see about Mother and Terry."

"Dad wants to see Joe."

"Can I go in too? I haven't seen him yet."

"Yeah, sure. Five minutes. He should sleep."

"Fine. Would you tell Mark and Chuck that Grandpa's going to be okay? He is, isn't he, John?"

"Yep. He's going to be all right. I'll call Barbara and Stephanie when we know something more."

Beverly took Joe toward the doors. She was whispering something to him, but he was not quite hearing it. She was saying something about Charlie wanting to pray, but Joe shouldn't do anything fancy, and he felt a strange urge to laugh. She was always telling him what to do. But something that had never happened to Joe began to happen to him. Everything seemed very distant and unreal. He felt like he was in a tunnel. He heard himself say "Hey, Charlie, heard you had quite a scare."

Beverly kissed her dad's brow. He had green tubes in his nostrils, an IV, and a catheter. His eyes were teared in the corners and his breathing was a little labored, but all things considered, he didn't look too bad. She told him that the doctor said he would be fine, and while she was talking, Joe started talking. She looked at Joe. She knew something was wrong.

Joe spoke too loudly, for one thing. For another thing, his face was positively white and there was sweat on his forehead. His hands were locked around the bed rail and his knuckles were bleached white. She walked around the bed to Joe's side and put her hand over one of his. He was clammy. "Joe?" she whispered.

"Don't you worry about anything, Charlie. Everything is going to be fine now. You just relax, okay?"

His voice was loud and someone from the nurse's station shushed him up in just as loud of a voice. "Come on, Joe," she said, and to her father, "I'll be just outside, Daddy. I'll be back as soon as I can. Come on, Joe."

He let her lead him away like an invalid. He walked like a robot. "What is it, Joe?"

"My head. My ears are ringing. I have to sit... sit down."

"What is it?" she asked him again.

But Joe couldn't answer. He didn't know what it was. He had visited hospital rooms a million times; often he had gone into ICU. He had never had a problem before, yet he had never felt so terrible.

Fifteen minutes later Beverly stood with John just on the other side of the potted plants that divided the waiting area from the elevators and hallway just outside ICU. They both looked into the little U-shaped arrangement of couches and chairs.

"I have never seen anything like it," she said.

Joe held an ice pack on the back of his neck. Terry's head was leaned back against the wall, the basin still firm in her hands on her lap. Delores had her head down, clutching her ammonia capsules in a trembling hand, her crunched-up handkerchief in the other.

"Chain reaction," John said. "Happens all the time. One of them goes and they all go."

Mark and Chuck were totally still, watching. They weren't even that quiet when they were asleep, Beverly thought.

"Come on," she said to John.

"No kidding. Dad's doing better than the rest of them."

"What do you think I ought to do with them?"

"Well, I think you ought to get them out of here."

"One at a time, or as a group?"

"Maybe you can get them to all hold hands or something. Come on, I'll help you."

Once they were all out of the hospital, in the crisp March air, recovery was almost instantaneous. Terry shook off the nausea and said she was hungry. Delores cried a little, but wanted to go home to call her other daughters. And Joe was a little embarrassed; he had had a flashback of some kind—something that had never happened to him before. He went with Beverly to her house, accepted a shot of brandy and a shoulder rub. Mark and Chuck started yelling again. By 7:00 P.M. things were nearly normal. Beverly wanted to go back to the hospital, so Joe baby-sat.

Charlie looked a little grayish. His breathing, however, had a normal sound. She touched his hand and he awoke.

"Hi, honey," he said weakly.

She kissed him gently. "Don't talk, Dad. Just rest."

"How's Mother?"

"Mother's fine. Hush now."

"Joe?"

How could he have noticed? He should be too sick to notice. "He's fine, Dad."

"Did you... did you get everyone settled?"

"Everyone is fine." She laughed softly. "Well, actually, you're doing better than everyone else. But you're not supposed to exert yourself. You'd better be quiet, or they'll throw me out."

"It's only the medicine. They're giving my heart a rest, but my heart is going to be fine. I'm probably going to have a bypass operation. John says it works real good."

"Good, Dad. That's good."

"Are you okay, honey?"

"Sure, Dad. I'm fine. You don't have to worry about me."

"I never did, honey. I never worried about you. Mother does all the worrying in our family."

"Yes." She laughed. "Yes, she does, doesn't she?"

"Thank you, honey. You take care of everything... everybody. Not much of a life for you, sometimes, I guess. But I'm proud of you, honey."

Beverly felt tears come to her eyes. She had never felt so close to her father before.

"Maybe you should go fix Joe some chicken soup or something. He looked pretty bad."

"I gave him a drink," she said, her voice quivering.

Charlie made a sound that was like a laugh. "Good," he said. "Good for you. Don't give him too much; preachers have no tolerance."

"I know. I told him that."

"You tell 'em, honey."

"I love you, Daddy."

"Yep. I'm a lucky man."

"I'm going to go so you can sleep."

"Okay, honey. Don't take any wooden nickels."

She said something like a prayer on the way home. Actually, it was more of a question. Is it time? she asked. For him? He should have a little time left, shouldn't he? At least he got his kids raised. There were a lot of things she hadn't told him yet. A lot of things he should know—like about the prom. She wanted to ask him if he remembered the prom. It hadn't gone very well; she hadn't been asked to go. And he took her to a sad movie—so she could have an excuse to cry. She refused to cry about a stupid old prom, but her dad knew that she really needed a good cry.

They couldn't let him down, she thought. He had gotten them raised and they had to let him know they were okay.

She walked into her quiet house. Obviously the boys had been put to bed. The living room was dark and the television was turned way down, low, so they could sleep. Joe was sitting on the couch, and she saw someone else that shouldn't be let down.

"I'm sorry," he said. "I wasn't exactly there when you needed me."

"You can't be every time."

"You were there for me though."

"Good. You can't have all the fun, you know."

And there was more truth in her words than she realized at that moment.

Nine

The most remarkable thing in the entire world must be bypass surgery. Charlie went home within ten days of his admittance, and in better shape than ever. The day after the surgery he was up and walking. Two weeks after the surgery he was home. He had a new diet, a few pills to take, an exercise routine to follow, and the doctor was going to let him go back to work part-time in six weeks. Even Delores, who loved to worry, settled down.

April came and the snow melted. So did Bev. A little. She could say "I love you" to Joe without looking devastated. She was saying it with a smile now and then. To the congregation at Joe's church she wouldn't confirm or deny any specific relationship. She admitted to liking Joe yet steadfastly promised never to marry him. She would not ever be a minister's wife. So she joined the Bible study and started helping Joe with the youth group. Beverly wasn't very convincing.

Beverly let April turn into a month of debates. She didn't always agree with Joe and was amazed that he didn't seem to expect her to. In fact, he seemed to encourage her own ideas. But she didn't buy it yet. She wouldn't pray with him.

In private she tried it out. You could get out of practice with that sort of thing. She only needed a sign.

A minor miracle would clinch it. She didn't consider the current happiness in her life to be any special favor. That was Joe. And Joe was mortal.

Beverly admitted to Joe that she didn't think they could make it together. They were too different. She liked a stiff drink and sex that wasn't sacred. She didn't ask him if that mattered, she just assumed it would. After all, he was a minister. Wow.

Joe checked with her from time to time to see if she was making any progress. He was only in a hurry, he explained, because being with her all the time and not being married to her was extremely hard on his nerves.

But Beverly didn't want to change her life. She lived a good life, did not commit any really serious sins; well, so what if she said damn a lot? Damn was a damn good word if you wanted the meaning of something to really stick, right? But she stopped putting God in front of it without really noticing. Joe told her to shut up and listen and maybe she would find out that He didn't even have any changes in mind. And she said she didn't want to be spiritual and pure and dull. And he laughed.

Beverly quit smoking. It didn't have anything to do with God or with Joe. She quit because she wanted to quit. You couldn't smoke at church and she was spending so damn much time there, she had just about lost the habit. There were some definite changes in Beverly and everyone could see it but her. John was glad. Delores was elated. Terry was confused. That's when Terry called Joe.

"Sure, I can see you, Ter. What's up?"

"Listen, I've never done anything like this before. It's personal. I don't want anyone to know I called you."

"Fine. When do you want to come over?"

"Soon. As soon as possible. Before I lose my nerve."

Joe laughed. "Come on, Terry. You're not afraid of me, now, are you?"

"Terrified," she murmured just before hanging up.

Joe didn't usually borrow trouble, but Terry was special to him. He hoped it wasn't as bad as she made it sound. He didn't feel much better when she tapped lightly at the office door and stood there looking humble and scared.

"Okay, Terry, why don't you tell me what's got you so upset?"

"I don't want to anymore. I think I want to leave. I'll sort this out on my own, okay?"

"Okay. You know my number."

"Okay, see ya."

"Bye."

"Joe?"

"Present."

"I don't know what to do."

"Neither do I. Want to talk?"

"No. No. I want to get out of here. Fast."

"I won't grill you, Terry. Let's talk about something else. Something not personal. School. How's school?"

Tears. Instant tears. Jackpot.

"The problem is school?" Joe couldn't hide his shock. Terry was a straight A student. Brilliant. She had a great future.

"Sort of. I'm all mixed up. The problem is... Joe, can I ask you something personal?"

"Sure. I don't know if I'll answer, but you can ask."

"Do you love Beverly?"

"Yes," he said with a big grin. "Yes, I do."

"Do you sleep with her?"

"That is a little personal. Very." She dropped her head, ashamed. It was personal, but then, so was her problem. "No, Terry. I guess what you want to know is if Bev and I have a sexual relationship and the answer is no. Not that I'm entirely happy about it."

"So, you really want to?"

"Now, that is personal. Too personal. Sorry, honey, but that's between me and Bev. I don't see what the answer to that could mean to anyone else. My business and my problem. Altogether too personal."

"You might have just said yes. It would have been a lot less windy in here."

"Yeah, I guess so." He shrugged. "So, what does that have to do with you?"

She raised her chin a notch. "I'm sleeping with Steve." She held her head high, daring him. Challenge. Terry wanted to fight it out. If Joe would be tough and unreasonable, she could run away and do as she pleased.

"So?"

"So? What do you mean, so? It's a sin."

"I don't think you came here to tell me that. We're not Catholics. You don't have to confess to me."

"Well, what do you have to say about it?"

"Nothing. Now, what's the problem?"

"I thought you would make a problem out of that."

"My job isn't making problems. And you just told me you were sleeping with Steve, which doesn't sound anything like a problem. That sounds like you've made up your mind. Did you expect me to try to talk you out of doing it again?"

"I know I'm going to do it again."

"Then why are you here? To ask me if I'm sleeping with Bev?"

"No."

"Then why?"

"Because I don't feel good. I need something. Because I know it isn't wrong, yet it still doesn't feel right. What kind of minister are you anyway?"

"Now I know the problem. Here, blow your nose. Take it easy."

"So what can you do?"

"What you want me to do. Talk this over with you. Sensibly."

"It won't help."

"Why don't you wait and see." This whole family, Joe thought, is in such a blasted hurry all the time. And plain unreasonable too. "Why don't you give me something to work with here? Tell me if you love him, how this got started, where you want to go with it."

"Of course I love him. What does that have to do with sin and sex and feeling bad?"

"Not a heck of a lot, unfortunately. So, what do you want to do about it?"

"We want to get married and we can't. Our parents are paying tuition and they both have decided that the financial help will stop if we get married before we graduate. They say if we love each other, we'll wait. We didn't tell them that we already haven't waited. We couldn't make it, Joe. We can't say it makes more sense to quit school. This time it sounds like it makes more sense to make love on the sly and stay in school."

"It sure does."

"You agree?"

"No. I said it sounds like that."

"Steve has talked about quitting school and working for a year or so, long enough to get us started. We've both applied for scholarships and financial aid programs, but aren't having much luck. I'm the one with the shot at a scholarship or aid, and poor Steve—well, his family has plenty of money. He has only one year left, Joe. And I'm not even halfway through. I'm afraid if I quit, I'll never go back, and if Steve doesn't finish for some reason... Oh, we want to be together, and we couldn't wait. We tried. It was just too painful."

"But you're not happy now, either, so it didn't solve much."

"Oh, Joe, you're wrong. It solved almost everything. We're happier, less frustrated, we even get more studying done. No doubts about anything anymore."

Joe had a flicker of recognition. Was even Terry, who had never been married, concerned about the sexual shape of her future marriage? Was bad sex that common? He had trouble relating. The worst sex he'd ever had was terrific.

"But it isn't enough and I'm moving in with Steve. I told my parents I'm taking an apartment with a girlfriend, but I'm really moving into Steve's place. I'm determined to do it, but the tension is killing me. I'm worried they'll find out and be crushed. Make a whole scene. But it isn't enough to keep me from doing it. Okay, Joe, do your stuff. Talk me out of it. And hurry. I'm packing."

"I can't. You don't want to change your mind."

"Do you have any alternatives?"

"Yes, get married anyway. Tell your parents the truth about your intentions and do what you have to do to be together and feel right about it. There is nothing wrong with your love for each other, but there's something really dangerous about deception and fear and torment."

"We've talked to our parents about wanting to get married. They won't budge. They don't believe we're capable of this kind of decision at our ages. They think we're too young. It seems to be a test of some kind, a test in the form of punishment. They're willing to pay tuition, but only on their terms. They think they're protecting us from making a big mistake or something."

"Of course they do, Terry, and you have to understand that. Their motives are the purest. The younger the marriage, the higher the risk of divorce, statistically. Keep yourself from getting mad, keep your perspective. Parents feel an overwhelming responsibility to share in this kind of decision-making. I'm sure if they had a crystal ball that proved your marriage would last in spite of your youth, they'd okay it. Right now they're scared to take that kind of chance."

"Understanding that doesn't help me."

"It might." Joe was a little puzzled, which wasn't unusual. There was no need to quote Scripture; Terry would know all the right passages. And she could know as well now as next year if she loved Steve enough to marry him. She was bright, mature, and had that good old healthy need. The bothersome one.

"I wonder. Terry, look, would you give me a little time to see if I can think of a better solution? I'd like to have a few facts and then see you and Steve together. What's his major?"

"Hospital administration."

"Doing well?"

"Real well. Three point two."

"And you're still in liberal arts, right?"

"So far."

"Okay, now, come back in a couple of days. Friday. And bring Steve. How about two o'clock?"

"Steve doesn't know I came to see you, Joe. I don't want to make him mad. We don't discuss our personal relationship with—"

"I'm not going to discuss sex. That's your business. Just bring him."

"Okay, but don't get me into trouble."

"Um, Terry?"

"Huh?"

"If you're so sure, so decided, why the tears?"

"I like you, Joe. You're good. It mattered. I didn't want you to be ashamed of me."

"Ashamed of you? Oh, honey, I couldn't be that." Joe rose from behind his desk and moved toward Terry. Terry, like Beverly, was going to cry some more. And Joe was going to hold her and tell her it was all right and that he understood, because he did.

Actually, Joe hadn't had a course on weeping women in the seminary. But he had done some homework on temptation, all kinds, and he knew something about that. He also knew when to pray and when to use his brain. He was a multifaceted preacher.

"What are you going to do, Joe?"

"See if I can find a way for you and Steve to keep sleeping together."

"Is that any way for a minister to talk?"

"I think you'll sleep a lot better with God's blessing, right?"

"I think so. I don't know."

"I know."

Terry went out with a sniff and Joe got on the phone. He had a nice talk with John, a nice talk with Charles Sullivan, the pastor and head honcho of the church, a nice talk with the administrator of student affairs at the college, and a not so nice talk with a bank officer.

"But I don't owe anybody any money. Why can't I co-sign a loan?"

"Because, Reverend, you don't have a credit rating."

"But I have a savings account. Number four two six eight seven three four nine oh eight."

"A very small savings account."

"Well, shit."

"What?"

"Look, the guy is real dependable, hard-working, pulling great grades in school. I have him all lined up with a good part-time job that will turn into full-time after graduation if he does well. It's not a gamble at all. I swear."

He thought the banker might say, "We already know you swear," but he just said, "Probably wouldn't be good enough. Sorry."

"Listen, could a single woman who is not a relative co-sign?"

"Anyone who qualifies can co-sign, Reverend."

Well, Beverly lived frugally, but Beverly was loaded. She didn't act loaded, but there was a healthy trust for the boys, more insurance on top of that, and a lawsuit with the trucking firm that had paid off right away. And social security. And she bought the duplex rather than renting. Cash.

Beverly didn't have many bills and she had a ton of charge accounts. She was sitting pretty, thanks to Bob's careful planning. Educations were set, there would always be plenty to eat, and beyond that Joe didn't know the bottom line. He thought it would be pushy to ask.

But now he had a good reason to ask.

"I know the kid personally, Bev. He's a fair risk. I wouldn't even ask you if I thought there was any chance he wouldn't make good. I'm willing to share responsibility with you. I made that offer to the bank, but they don't trust me."

"Well, if you think it's safe and he's in need, why don't you let me make him a loan? He can pay me back at a little lower interest rate. I can spare it."

"That's nice, but remember, honey, this is a business proposition only. He didn't ask for any favors. I don't want to bruise his pride."

"It's on your conscience, big boy."

"I love you."

"I know. You said that already."

"Can I come over tonight?"

"No."

"Why not?"

"Because I have never been invited to your place. It's rude. Very tacky too."

"Worried?"

"Ha-ha. Got a roommate you don't want me to meet?"

"I'll make you and the boys some hot dogs on my grill if it doesn't rain and you can check out my bachelor pad. How about six o'clock?"

"See you then, preacher baby."

She was dynamite. Sexy and wild. Beautiful. He asked again: Wouldn't it be all right just once? Just once and I won't do it again until she marries me? One night? Please?

No.

That's what I thought. Don't get sore, I'm only checking. Amen.

Joe believed that God had a good sense of humor. There was time enough for all the serious praying, time for holiness and righteousness, and in his spare time he talked to his good friend, his Holy Father. God would never have let the world exist this long if He were short on patience or tolerance. That was what the Son was for. Anyway, Joe figured God was getting a real kick out of his control. Control? Something like that.

While he was praying more earnestly for Beverly's soul, really giving it the old concentration and urgently pleading. He was also doing a lot of complaining about his waning resistance. "See, it's like this, Lord—I just don't think I can take any more of those dreams. I really am getting too old for that kind of thing. Beverly is about to hit her prime and I'm about to lose mine. Now, if we're going to have a baby together, we had better get married and she won't marry me until she stops thinking I'm on some kind of crazy God trip. And about temptation, well, you just don't know temptation until you start hanging around with Beverly. And about that baby, I'd like a girl. Amen."

Joe admitted to Beverly that he hadn't rushed home to clean his apartment. He didn't have to. He was fussy, neat, and tidy. It wasn't much either. Clean as a whistle, sparsely furnished, and small. Very small. One whole room.

"Tell the truth, Joe, the only reason you want to get married is so you can move into a bigger place, right?"

"Right. Right into your place."

"Forget it. When am I going to meet this kid? The one who wants me to co-sign his loan?"

"Well, you'll meet him if he lets you. See, I promised I wouldn't give the kids away. They're trying to work out some sticky problems right now. You know how it is with kids, Bev. They're in love."

"Why the big secret? Are they in trouble?"

"No, nothing like that. They just can't afford to get married and stay in school too. I'm trying to find a way for both."

"Think you can?"

"I think I did. If they like the idea, that is."

"That fast? They can't be very bright or they would have done it themselves."

"They were too scared. They thought maybe it would be easier to skitter around the problem in devious ways rather than facing up to what they have to do. I think kids have problems because they feel like puppets with their parents, teachers, and ministers pulling the strings. They try to beat the folks at the parent game, and end up avoiding all the real issues. You know, if they didn't have parents to argue with, they would have found their own solutions eventually. And they don't have as many problems as they think they have. They ought to make it, no sweat."

"I have no idea what you're talking about."

"Well, never mind. I do. Are you free Friday?"

"Not until four, why?"

"I'm meeting with them again, and if they like my idea, maybe you could come over and meet them. How's that?"

"I'll call you when the fashion show is over and if you want me to come then, I will."

Joe thought that would be great. He thought Terry and Steve would be relieved. They would prefer to be honest, make it right, without lying or playing games.

When Friday rolled around, Joe was a little surprised to find that Steve was aware of what Terry had said two days earlier. For some reason Joe thought Terry might keep it from Steve, skirt the issue a little, hold back. Joe was glad she hadn't. He felt a new respect for their love. He thought they would make it just fine. Steve was the first to speak.

"We've done a lot of talking about this, Joe, and I guess I wasn't paying attention. Terry has been upset and I've been so anxious to have her with me that I didn't even notice. She's not moving in with me. We're getting married. I'm going to drop out of school for a while and work full-time. I can still take a few classes. We couldn't handle the deception."

"I think I have a better idea," Joe said. "I think I found a way for you to get married and stay in school. I want to make it perfectly clear to you both that I wouldn't have gotten involved if you had been minors. But you're both legally adults and I believe it's to your definite advantage to play the game straight from the start—and continue your education as well. I'll be pleased to explain my interference to your parents, even if they're not very understanding."

Joe amazed them with his facts and figures. He had Terry all lined up with a good summer job that could turn into part-time work in the fall. He was putting her in the church office with Reverend Sullivan and he would hire the other secretary. The pay wasn't great, but it was flexible and long-term. And there would be light days when she could study on the job.

Steve was to go to the county hospital and see the administrator the following Monday. If he passed the civil service test, which should be a snap, he would have a full-time summer job and part-time job in the fall. The hospital administrator was receptive to the idea that there might be a full-time position available for Steve after he graduated. It might take him a while to become a full-fledged administrator, but he had the opportunity to prove himself.

Next, Joe explained the loan. It would pay both tuitions for one year. They would have to feed themselves, pay their rent, and whatever else was necessary to live. According to the budget he had drawn up, he couldn't see why they would have any real problem. It would be a little tight, but it was always a little tight. There was even a column for the church; he had arranged a pittance for their tithing. Joe was relentless.

"There's another problem, Terry and Steve, and it doesn't have anything to do with money. It isn't going to be easy for both of you to work and go to school. You'll be too tired, sometimes, to enjoy all that great legal sex. You'll feel the pressure, be pressed to find time to be together. You may even have trouble talking, yet you will have made serious promises to each other. Living together is tough even when things are easy. You're not going to have it easy. Are you sure?"

"We're sure," Steve said. "We can't put it off any longer."

"When?"

"As soon as possible. My roommate can move into the frat house and Terry can move in with me. No big deal, just simple and legal. And soon."

"What's the rush?"

"Come on, Joe."

"Okay, do you want to get married here?"

"Only if you'll do it. And soon."

Kids. Always in a hurry. Slow down, kids. It isn't that perfect even when it's legal. It will be blessed, but that doesn't mean it will be ideal. There will be trouble with the folks even with the preacher on your side. Even with all the help in the world, marriage is tough. Pray, love, cooperate, share. And slow down.

"We want to write our own vows, Joe. Will you help?"

"I have some very definite ideas about what marriage means as a commitment, Terry and Steve. You may want to hear me out and then decide if you want my help. I could be considered very old-fashioned. Some people have even accused me of being on a God trip."

Well, they were pretty excited, but they could sit still long enough to listen to Joe when he talked about his personal impressions of lifetime contracts. They were a little worried about their parents and they all had a good laugh about how surprised Beverly was going to be when she found out that Steve and Terry were the ones who needed a loan. They didn't laugh over that for long. Beverly blew in like a hurricane. Actually, she moved in like a thundercloud that was about ready to burst.

"These are the young people? My own sister."

"Then you've met?"

"Why didn't you tell me?"

"What happens in my office is none of your business."

"Even when it's my own family?"

"Especially then. It is always confidential here. Always."

"That's a lousy excuse. You should have told me anyway."

"What's the difference? I'm telling you now."

"Your idea is all wet too. I will not co-sign a bank loan; not for my own sister."

"Don't you think you ought to ask them what they want? Or do you already have all the answers?"

"Hey, don't get uppity with me, Joseph. If they need money, I can give them money."

"Beverly, just slow down here. They didn't ask you for—"

"They didn't ask the right person, that's what. If you'd been thinking, you would have told Terry to just come to me and—"

"I didn't tell Terry anything. That isn't my job. You like to tell people what to do and I like to encourage them to—"

"At the very least, you should have told me my sister had some kind of a problem so I could—"

"This may come as a big shock to you, Beverly, but not everyone likes it when you take charge of their lives. Terry might have preferred to work this out her own way."

"But she didn't, did she? She's getting to work it out your way."

"What are you, jealous? Jealous because—"

"Don't you dare yell at me."

"You're yelling. Not me. You haven't even taken the time to listen to what's been going on here; you're so busy taking over. Why don't you settle down and listen to what they have in mind?"

"Because all that business about the hard times is a lot of crap and I don't want my own sister drudging through her last years of school and first years of marriage with nothing but money worries. If they need money, I want to help."

"Why don't you shut up and let them speak for themselves. Just for once, Beverly, shut up."

"Don't you tell me to shut up, you—"

"Beverly, I swear, I never wanted to belt a woman before I met you."

"Try it once, Clark!"

Terry and Steve stared at them in silent wonder while they brawled. Joe and Beverly were oblivious to the young couple. They were having a fight. Joe was used to this. Beverly liked to fight and call names and yell. She thrived on it. And Beverly also liked to win all the fights, even if she was wrong. Maybe one reason she was yelling was that she couldn't think straight, her mind was so boggled with figures and investments and interest rates. Beverly had confided that she was rich. Really loaded. If she never remarried, she could probably maintain a comfortable living till she was one hundred and ten years old. Beverly wanted to pay off Terry and Steve and buy them a "happily ever after marriage." She wanted to be the one responsible.

Beverly, bless her, could be a real pain in the ass.

Joe strode toward Beverly and really wanted to hit her, just to shut her up. Once she got her wind up, you couldn't get a word in edgewise with Beverly. There was no reasoning with her. He shut her up by kissing her hard.

"Beverly, will you be quiet?"

"I hate you."

"Sure." He kissed her again. And again. Finally, her arms went around his neck. There was one thing Beverly liked better than yelling, and that was kissing Joe. He was nearly expert at kissing her by now. And he was getting pretty good at shutting her up too.

"Okay, you win. I'll shut up."

"Well, thank God."

"Stop all that praying. Do you want to come over tonight?"

"Are you going to behave yourself?"

"Do you want me to?"

"I'd better stay home and watch the ballgame."

"I'll be good."

"That's what I'm afraid of. I'll watch the ballgame."

"Watch it at my house, with the boys..."

Terry and Steve had seen the Reverend Clark and Mrs. Simpson kiss before. They were steadies now. They were together at family gatherings and at church. They were together more than they were apart. They were the talk of the town, Joe obviously in love and asking Beverly to marry him almost daily and Beverly obviously in love and refusing constantly. Half the congregation had started a pool, placing bets on who would win this little war.

Joe would win the battle. Beverly shut up and loaned Steve the money on his terms, with low interest and easy payments while he was in school and larger payments after graduation. The foursome faced Terry's parents and found little resistance there. They finally came around willingly and offered to continue to help with Terry's tuition for a while.

Steve's parents were another story. They were angry with Steve, Joe, Terry, and even Beverly. But the kids faced them bravely, told them the truth, and Steve kept his cool. Steve told his parents that he hoped they would come to understand his situation in time and he apologized if he had hurt them. He would marry Terry in any case, and he was incredibly mature at that moment.

Joe had heard about confused youth, about their total disregard for religious commitment and their rebellious natures. There were many times Joe couldn't help. Even more were the times his help was never sought. And there were countless times his offered help was rejected, refused. Joe was feeling good. Not because he was able to help Terry. Because she had asked.

"I'm sorry I was so bossy," Beverly said. She snuggled up to Joe after the ballgame, after the boys went to bed. "Are you mad at me?"

"Nope. I pretty much expected it."

"Oh, you did, did you? What are you? Psychic?"

"Yeah, sure." He laughed. As if a person had to be psychic to expect Beverly to get bossy.

"I think I was jealous," she said. "I wish they had come to me. Anyway, whatever the reason, I let it irritate me and make me unreasonable, bossy, and mean."

"It's okay, honey. I understand."

"You do?"

"Sure." He was going to explain it to her, but she snuggled closer and he didn't feel like talking. Later, though, when he could think clearly again, he remembered. It was like this with Beverly. She could love with such intensity, she sometimes scared herself. Often, he suspected her bossiness, humor, stubbornness, and good old fighting spirit were more to let off steam because what she felt inside was so strong. And Beverly loved Terry and Steve like crazy. Had they gone to her instead of Joe, she might have gone overboard with them. She might have given them the money too easily and robbed them of the chance to dig into their own hearts for their answers.

Beverly's reactions were sometimes a little radical, but her heart was solid gold.

$\mathcal{T}en$

$\mathcal{J}$oe asked Delores when Bob had died. The exact date. "Why?" she asked.

"I don't know. I've never been this close to a widow before. I just thought I should know, be ready or something."

"You've been really good to her, Joe. I really appreciate it."

Delores was probably sincere in saying that, but Joe sometimes felt cheated. He wanted a little more from Beverly than he was getting. He wanted her to drop her guard a little, trust herself a little more. Joe already knew she trusted him. She was still awfully scared of herself though. Scared she would guess wrong, decide wrong, or commit wrong. For now he was being rewarded by the sound of her laughter instead of her tears. Bev could deny him, denounce him, run from him, and fight him. But she loved him and she was happy. Someday she would run out of excuses to keep herself away from him. Joe hoped and prayed that he could outlast her.

When Terry and Steve met with Joe to set the date and make some definite plans, they suggested May 7. Joe asked if there was any other date they could agree on and they asked him why. So that was how it was. No one really remembered. Bob Simpson was dead and buried and Joe Clark was considered his replacement. That's what everyone thought, apparently. Everyone but Beverly. Joe knew that Bev hadn't forgotten. She wouldn't forget for a long time.

"Because that's the day that Bob died. It might be easier on Bev if you chose another day. "She wouldn't ask you, but I am."

"I feel like a dog," Terry muttered.

"Well, don't. You're not supposed to dwell on it. The date is unimportant; the memory of a fine man is. Bev doesn't need a calendar to miss Bob. I just have a feeling she'll know. Just a feeling."

So they moved the wedding date up a week. Naturally. They couldn't wait. May first was the big day. There was a fever in the air whenever Terry and Steve were around. Joe suspected they had decided to abstain until the vows were exchanged, but asking would be getting downright ridiculous about the whole thing.

But not for Beverly. Besides being a regular pain, she was nosy. She couldn't stand being left out of a secret.

"Tell me which one of them approached you, at least," she begged.

"Nevermind."

"Come on."

"Forget it, Beverly, I'm not telling you."

"Well, why not?"

"Top secret. And none of your business."

"They're getting married. It's no secret now."

"Leave it alone, Beverly. I'm not telling you."

"Did they tell you they were sleeping together?"

"They were? Oh, God!"

"It happens, you know." Beverly the wise.

"It's going to happen to you, too, if you don't put on some clothes."

Beverly stood her ground. She let Joe admire her short shorts while she cleaned the patio door. There was a lot of bending, stretching, and leaning involved in cleaning a sliding glass door. Bev had nice legs, a nice posterior, and Joe suspected everything else was nice too. He was starting to bead with sweat.

"Why don't you wear jeans? I love the way you look in jeans."

"It's too hot for jeans."

"Beverly, why don't you just marry me? I can't take this anymore."

"Nope."

"Then will you make me some iced tea?"

"Why can't you make it yourself?"

"Because if I try to stand up I'm going to break something."

Just this once she would make it for him. When men started asking you to wait on them, and started dropping by in the middle of the day because they were in the general area (about fifteen miles away), things were getting a little too heavy. When she had wanted badly to get married, she and Bob had to wait. When she didn't want to get married at all, the eager-beaver preacher was asking her daily.

Yes, things were definitely getting too hot with the minister. Better break it off, Bev. Let him down nice and easy. Wouldn't want to hurt him; he's a nice guy. Nice guy: green light.

"Are you still taking out your laundry, Joe?"

"Well, I don't have time to do laundry and court the 'merry widow.'"

"You might as well bring it over here then. I have to do about ten loads a week anyway. I wouldn't mind."

"Really?"

"You know me. I'm not that generous."

"Okay, deal. I'll bring it over tonight."

And that was another thing. He was always inviting himself to dinner. And if he didn't, Beverly invited him.

"Come at five and have dinner. Macaroni and cheese."

"My favorite."

"Everything is your favorite. You're a kid in a man's body."

"Can I have a hot dog with my macaroni and cheese?"

Joe didn't mean to be adorable. That was something that just sort of happened whenever he was honest. He was cute. He was cute as long as you listened to him and kept from looking at him. When you looked at him, it did something to your heart. Beverly could look over the length of him, some six feet plus, and get just plain weak. She had seen a high school picture of him once and laughed until he was ready to smack her. He had been kind of homely, lanky and spindly-looking with sandy hair and freckles. No more.

For the next twelve or so years after high school he had kept active athletically and had lived in some interesting separate worlds. There was that very important straight world that he'd lived in the majority of his life, and then there was the period of three or four years that she called his "sin trip." During that time he had done everything. He wouldn't say exactly what, just everything.

Maybe it was that time period that gave his eyes such a look of depth and wisdom. Beverly wouldn't ever really know. But all those years added up to a man who was strong, sure, confident, and beautiful. Not simply physically, but in his mind, his will. It was something Bev had grown to admire.

The big day for the wedding was fast approaching. Delores would have a houseful. Bev's two sisters, Stephanie and Barbara, would come to the wedding with their husbands and children and stay with Delores. Bev wasn't close to these two sisters, but they were close to each other. Bev seemed to be closer to Terry and John. Things worked like that in families. They were all perfectly content with the way things had turned out.

There was something else that was unusual, or at least uncommon about this family. Joe noticed it as others had.

"You know, Bev, your sisters are all really pretty, your brother is a very handsome man, and it's no secret that I think you're a knockout."

"Thanks."

"No, I mean, you're welcome, but that's not what I mean. What I mean is that your parents aren't... well, they're pretty ordinary-looking people. But their children are gorgeous. There's hardly any resemblance. Are you all adopted or something?"

She laughed. "No."

It was a common observation and very difficult to verbalize unless you were one of them. Beverly's parents were plain and had always been, even in youth. The children, however, were fine-looking. Very beautiful, in fact. It was the kind of thing people noticed when they saw the family together. Like it was the perfect combination of genes or something.

"But then, I'm not a bad-looking guy and you're gorgeous. Do you think that means we'd have an ugly baby?"

"Want to check it out, Rev?"

"Knock it off, Beverly."

Beverly was making herself useful by butting into all Terry's plans, trying to make everything perfect. Terry hadn't given much notice, but that didn't stop Bev. She insisted on a shower, a party, and other affairs that Terry would have passed up. In the meantime, her curiosity was killing her. Terry had mentioned that she and Steve had written their own vows and Joe had helped. Terry wouldn't tell her what they would say and neither would Joe. All Joe would admit to was including some Christian attitudes toward commitment, and some doctrine on the marriage contract.

That was that. Beverly had to wait. Now, Beverly might be a lot of things, but she definitely was not dumb. Steve and Terry had come to admire Joe with a kind of passion. Indeed, they might have written their own vows, but much of what they said to each other was bound to be from Joe. He had a way of making a person one of the flock.

May first did arrive, though Terry said often that she wondered if it ever would. She donned a long cream- colored dress and carried a bouquet of fresh flowers. She allowed Bev to fuss over her a little and Delores would not be stopped. Charlie led his youngest daughter down the aisle and handed her over to the groom. Terry was twenty years old. She didn't tremble or quiver. She was sure. Dead sure.

Beverly watched Joe more than the bride and groom. He stood before them in a nice suit instead of the robes he usually wore at worship. Since Terry and Steve were keeping it simple, he suggested that he do the same.

Oh, Beverly watched Joe, but Joe did not watch Bev. He was in charge up there; completely absorbed. He talked quietly to Terry and Steve, smiling occasionally as if they were telling jokes, and then he closed his eyes and said a prayer with them. It all seemed a very private affair. Beverly should have tried to catch a few words, she was close enough, but she was spinning with thoughts, many of which had to do with the handsome sandy-haired preacher.

Joe was special. It wasn't a personal opinion by a long shot. Everyone thought so. Because it was true. The entire congregation adored him. He was gifted. Also, he was friendly, kind, tolerant, thoughtful, and funny. He made people laugh at him, at themselves, at life, at love, and even at sin. He was very nearly perfect. He was not unlike Bob. A girl could do worse, but Bev just wasn't sure. Too many experiences had shaped her into the person she was now. She thought she might really have a screw loose.

When you've watched the man you love die, had an affair with one of his best friends, been attacked by various sex maniacs, tried to seduce a homosexual, and topped it off by tempting a man of the cloth, you had to be a bit dotty. And still trying to make something real out of your life certainly meant the psyche was damaged. She didn't want to mess up what was left of her life by entering into something with doubts. If she had earned nothing else from her pain, she had at least earned the right to be careful. Loving Joe was something she simply couldn't help.

"Friends," the assistant minister said, "this man and woman come to God's house today to pledge themselves to each other in marriage. They have exchanged the marital promises you are accustomed to hearing. They have bowed their heads before our Lord to ask for this Divine blessing on this union. Now they invite us to share and witness their special words of promise to each other as they seal their vows."

Terry and Steve turned around to face the congregation. It was an intimate group that attended them that day. They were bright, happy, and in love. Tears came to Beverly's eyes. About fourteen years ago another young couple faced the gathering in the church. They were also bright, happy, and in love. They were filled with hope and optimism. They were no more.

Terry said: "Loved ones, I have come here today to give myself in marriage to Steve. I give myself before God for the sake of love and hope. I commit myself to Steve with the promise that I will stay faithful to my husband and my promises, share his dreams and desires, support him in all things, and for all time. I pledge myself in hope: hope for the future, for the fruits of our union, and hope for the strength to do God's will in my marriage and in my life."

Steve said: "While I pledge all this to my love, Terry, we add to this a prayer. We pray that God gives us the strength to be steadfast to Him and each other, to follow His will as a family, to follow the path He plans for us without straying, to live with His purpose as we endeavor to live by His Holy Law. We ask that you, our loved ones, pray for us as we seek peace and happiness through our marriage and our lives."

Bev didn't hear the rest. She was brushing little tears from her eyes and sniffing. So, that was Joe. And now it was Terry and Steve. They would promise to live with a commitment to each other while simultaneously making a commitment to their faith. And sealed in the name of Jesus Christ while she was blowing her nose.

No small thing, this getting married, if you listened to the words. An awful lot of promising for two kids who had just been fooling around. But the words had fallen on many ears and everyone but Beverly was making their way to the altar to kiss the bride and groom. So, finally, Bev went too. She kissed the bride, the groom, and the minister. Pretty sloppy wedding, all in all.

"You win, Joe. I don't know what good it did, but I said a prayer."

"What did you pray?"

"I prayed that they never have to suffer or put up with any shit. I prayed that they can live together forever and never have to know the misery of betrayal, loss, death, or longing. And I prayed really hard too."

"That's great, Bev, we're making progress. Now, why don't you change that prayer just a little bit?"

"Why? It was a damn good prayer."

"I know. But it might go down just a little better if you said something more like what you want, and then, 'Let Your will be done and give them the strength, courage, and faith to live with it.'"

"Do you really think He'd like that better?"

"Yes, I think so."

"You're a damn know-it-all. I don't know if I want to change it to that. I'll have to think about it."

"Good, you think. I'm going to have some wedding cake."

Beverly changed the prayer. A little. "God, give them the strength, courage, and faith to live with Your decisions, but please, please, don't screw it up for them. Amen."

Steve and Terry went off to have their honeymoon, and they went with glad hearts, and even Beverly the logical and rational could see that. And Joe was invited to take Beverly and the boys home after the reception. That's when he hit her with the big question. Would she like to help him take a group of teenagers on a weekend camping trip in two weeks?

"Where do you come up with such things?"

"It was their idea. Are you game?"

"Are you going to behave yourself?"

"I generally do. You're the one with the shaky moral conduct."

"Don't be a smart-ass. I'll go if Mom will keep the boys."

"Well, I already talked to John about that. He and your dad are going fishing for the weekend and he'd like to take them along."

"Dad? Away for the weekend? What about his heart?"

"His doctor thinks it's a great idea. Real relaxing."

"Oh, sure. Mark and Chuck ought to relax him right into another heart attack."

"Naw," Joe said. "Look, this has been all checked out already. This is a certifiably good idea. Charlie wants to spend more time with his grandsons, John needs a break and can look after all of them just fine, and you should go along with this. Really."

"Let the boys go without me? Without my permission?"

"Preferably with your permission, and definitely without you. Your brother has a friend who has a well-furnished cabin on a lake. It's near a good hospital and there's nothing to worry about."

"Is this all arranged?"

"Sort of."

"I don't know." Beverly the mother started to twist her hands. "I haven't ever sent them on a fishing trip, or anything. What if something happens?"

"Your brother is a doctor and your father has raised five kids. What better credentials do you want?"

"I don't know if I'm ready for this."

"Well, get ready, Bev. Let go a little."

"Is my grip too tight?"

"Yes. A little. They already know they don't have a father; don't smother them. Ease up a little."

"Do you really think—"

"I think," he said, "that whenever you box someone in, it makes them want to bust out."

Bev let the boys plan it, and they were ecstatic. She could see their excitement as further proof that Joe was a natural at this sort of thing. He had an insight into children and young adults that went beyond the parent. The boys had their gear packed and waiting at Grandpa's house over a week before they were supposed to leave. Bev and Joe were going a half hour's drive across town and the boys would be all the way up north. Fishing. It might as well have been the moon.

They didn't make any plans for the weekend before that. Joe didn't ask her out and she didn't invite him over. She didn't tell the boys it had been exactly two years since their father had died, and she didn't tell Joe. She tried not to tell herself, but she already knew it.

She fed the boys early and turned on the TV. It wouldn't block out her thoughts. It was staying light out later and school would be over in a couple of weeks. She struggled against an odd urge and finally gave in, put on a reasonably clean sweatshirt, and piled the boys in the car.

She told them she would be running a short errand and they could plan the fishing trip with Grandpa while she was gone. They said that was okay. Grandma said it was okay, too, but only after a short investigation. So where was Beverly going? Just a short errand. And how was everything? Everything was fine, dandy in fact. She was to take her time, but Beverly said it wasn't apt to take long.

It wasn't likely the church would be unlocked, since there were no cars outside, but it was. And it wasn't very likely that the lights would be on, and they weren't. It was fairly dark. Dark enough to be a little scary if you couldn't see the doors from the altar. Bev would know if someone was locking up and there was always the phone, but she would die before she'd call Joe and tell him she was locked up in a church.

So, how do you go about this anyway? Maybe lighting some candles would help; it did wonders for the Catholics. It did seem to help. The flickering candles illuminated the church and made it come alive.

Okay, God. Do your stuff. I came here willingly. Hit me. It hasn't been all that bad lately, but that's Joe. He makes things seem better than they are. And I'm managing pretty well even if I don't have a natural flair for being both mother and father. If You do any thinking about Joe, however, please use Your head on this one and don't let him get his stupid heart broken over some dumb, maladjusted widow. Deal?

That's not it, though. However well I seem to manage and however much I seem to be leaning on Joe, I can't stop missing Bob. Oh, God, I still wait for him to come home in the evenings and reach for him in the night. I can feel love again and it's just not the same. It had finally become so solid and sure with Bob.

Now it's all second-hand. Everything I have to offer I have already given. No one will ever have me fresh and new and full of energy. I come now with a ready-made family and a stretched-out body. I don't want to start over. I want to go back. Back to Bob. Back to growing old with the man I love. Back to comfort and security.

Oh, God, here it comes. I'm trying, but I can't stop it. I need that strength and courage and faith and I need it fast. I need a way to forget. There were so many men who weren't loved by their families, who weren't so good and strong and decent, and it was my Bob You had to take. So why? Oh, God, why? What super plan couldn't have been worked out with him still alive? It was a dirty trick to yank him away and You know it. And he loved You. Worshiped You. And the suffering? What the hell was that for? My Bob, my good and decent and strong man... why, why, why?

It would always end that way. Beverly was overcome. Whenever she let herself remember her incredible pain, she simply couldn't bear it. She let her head drop down to the rail and she wept hard and bitter tears. Her back heaved and she snorted. Bev had never been a charming weeper. She was downright miserable at it.

And another thing—now she was never alone with her hateful tears. She could never just lay her head down and cry her heart out when she wanted to. Then there was a hand on her shoulder that she thought might be the hand of God reaching out to comfort her. She turned on that hand angrily, ready to push it away. Instead, she fell into the assistant minister's arms... like a bad habit.

"What are you doing here?" she choked out. "Did you follow me?"

"I was here when you came in. In the back. You didn't see me."

"Why didn't you say anything?"

"I was just going to go outside and wait for you. I'm sorry, Bev, I just couldn't leave you like this. I just had to hold you."

"You're a sucker for tears, huh?"

"Yep. Yours, anyway."

"So what are you doing here?"

"Same as you, I think."

"Which is?"

"Praying on the anniversary of Bob's death."

"Well, I think that takes a helluva nerve. You didn't even know him."

"No, but I've come to admire him a great deal; his memory at least. He must have been a fine man and I love his sons. I wanted to pray for you too, Bev. I really hoped you'd make it through this okay."

"Thanks, I guess." More tears. Well, it just couldn't be helped when you were busy drowning in self-pity. Even though it would have been nice to be left alone in private agony, it wasn't too hard to lean against Joe's chest and cry. She had already accustomed herself to the feel of that chest, the smell, and the arms that went around her which were secure and strong.

"Oh, Joe. He's gonna be so disappointed in me."

"Who?"

"Who do you think? The Boss."

"Why?"

"Because I came here to pray for strength and courage and all those virtuous things, and I ended up yelling at Him. Screaming at Him and calling Him names and blaming Him."

"It's okay, baby. You can get mad at God. He can take it."

"He's gonna be pissed. Hold a grudge. Cross me off the Big List."

"No."

"My debut, and I blew it."

"He loves you, Bev. No strings. You don't even have to love Him back."

"Bull. He's gonna be really pissed this time."

"You'll make up. He's not going anywhere."

She must have really been down because she sat there and listened to Joe for a long time even though her gut feeling was to run and hide. He had a different voice for her when he murmured words of condolence, promise, love, and blessing. It wasn't his pulpit voice, beautiful, but not pulpit. She even bowed her head and tried to pray with him, but she was still a little too mad for that. And she was sad, too, but not afraid anymore. Not with Joe there to act like a go-between for her and the Big Guy.

Though distraught and upset, she managed to allow him to kiss her a little, right in front of God and everything. It was like he was trying to show her here and now that she wasn't too far gone to feel, to tingle a little, to know a love that was fresh and new even if she wasn't. When she pressed this firm man, felt his tender touch and honest love, she could manage something other than despair.

When they walked out of the church into the crisp spring night, Beverly felt washed. Unloaded and lighter. She asked Joe to follow her home. She didn't want it to go away for a while.

Eleven

everly saw the boys off on their fishing trip. She let them skip school on Friday to leave early with Uncle John and Grandpa. The youth group was not allowed to skip school and she and Joe left with them Friday afternoon. Two other couples and a dog came along too.

The teenagers were so wound up and excited that you couldn't help but have fun. They pitched a tent for the old folks, got a fire going, and sang songs. Not hymns, but silly, stupid songs. The kind that made you laugh until you hurt. Of course, the kids didn't want to sleep—ever. They might just have the stamina to go all night, so Joe insisted that they lay their heads down and prepare to sleep under the stars. There was still a lot of monkey business, but Bev fell asleep anyway.

Sometime between moonlight and dawn they all got very, very wet. There was nothing to do but roll up the sleeping bags and gear and take off. That's exactly what they did, laughing like a bunch of happy-go-lucky idiots rather than bemoaning their lost weekend.

It was early Saturday by the time they got to Bev's house. She made Joe breakfast and they talked for a while about heading up north to join the other party. They didn't talk about it long. They both knew it was a bad idea. It was time for Bev to leave the boys alone for a weekend.

So Beverly and Joe took a nap. No funny stuff, just a nap. And they did Joe's laundry and straightened up the house. Then Bev remembered there was this leak and that crack and a screw loose in more than her head. Joe fixed everything.

When Beverly prepared dinner it was altogether too quiet in the house. Even Joe thought so, but he wouldn't let her cry. She had done more than enough crying and it was time for her to face the fact that the boys were growing up and would be around the house less and less.

Beverly turned on the stereo and then she turned to Joe. She reclined on the couch and he reclined on her. She savored the taste of his mouth; he delighted in hers.

It was all very nice and very natural and very familiar. When you had decided, as they had, to maintain this nice platonic relationship, you kissed until your mouth hurt and then you rolled away from each other and ached until you forgot why you were aching.

Completely unplanned and unprepared and unreasonable, Beverly pushed the preacher off her and bounded off the couch. That was usually his move, but tonight it was hers. And she was dead serious.

"Enough!"

"Okay. Don't get mad. You're right—"

"No, I mean enough of that crap forever. The end!"

"What?" Poor Joe. It was a shock to the system. He was in no condition for a fight.

"I mean that I am thirty-four years old and I was married for nearly twelve years and I'm sick of the frustration. I can't take it anymore, Joe. It's got to stop... or something."

"Okay, I vote for the 'or something.' Do you want to get married?"

"No!"

"Stop yelling. I can hear you already."

"I have to yell, it's how I'm made. Now, listen up, Joseph, and hear me out. All this necking is fine for the little teeny-boppers who don't know what they're doing or what's coming, but I'm a grown woman and the mystery was gone a long time ago. This frustration is eating me up. I am ready for a sexual relationship. Now!"

"Are you done yelling?"

"Yes."

"Good. I think we should wait."

"For what?"

"For a little something more than wanting to do it," he yelled back.

"I know you think that. It's like this, chum, I have my reasons for thinking waiting is absurd. I don't want to wait and I don't know when I'm going to be ready to get married. I want to know first if we're compatible, and if you can't agree to that, I don't want to see you anymore. I just can't handle this."

"I think if you're going to deliver ultimatums like that, I have a right to know the reasons."

"You won't judge me?"

"Have I ever?"

"Okay, but this is not easy. I had a good intimate relationship with Bob; we were compatible. We were compatible in a lot of ways and one of the most important ways was sexually. After Bob died I had an affair with a man I had known for years. Now, Joe, I didn't just fall into bed with the guy, but we ended up there and it was awful. Really nothing. Joe, I would have married him. I would have married him first if he had wanted that. And I would have followed widowhood with a divorce."

"So you want to see if I can deliver? Check me out?"

"Don't make it sound so cold. I love you, after all."

"You thought you loved him."

"I was wrong. Lonely. Desperate. Horny. Not now. Now I am sure about how I feel about you. But that won't make up for the loss if we can't... you know."

"And does that solve it then? If we go to bed and it all works out, then are we going to make a real commitment?"

"No deals, Joe. I don't know what this will solve besides getting rid of the frustration. When I'm ready for marriage again, I'll let you know. I'm not ready now."

"Okay, now calm down and think. What kind of guy was he? Could you tell by his character that he wouldn't be interested in pleasing you? Could you see that he wasn't the type to cooperate and try to work things out?"

"No. He courted me. Babied me. Mr. Congeniality before; a real pain afterward."

"Do you think I'll turn into a real pain afterward like he did?"

"No, but—"

"Say it, Beverly. The truth."

"It's ugly. Cold."

"Just say it."

"You're a preacher."

"Coward."

"Okay, so maybe preachers only do it one way. Maybe it's dull. Maybe they only do it on Saturdays. How would I know?"

"You could ask me. I love you, Bev. I don't advertise, but I wouldn't be opposed to a very frank and honest discussion with the woman I love and want to marry. I'll tell you how I feel and I won't lie. You can't marry me if you don't believe me and trust me—before and after."

"I've been through enough, Joe. I just can't make any mistakes now. It would finish me off. I have to be sure, really sure."

"And sex is the big issue, right?"

"Right now, yes."

"I must have missed a course somewhere. I never would have believed there was so much bad sex floating around. Is that the most important consideration?"

"Now. Right now it is the big issue. I'm sorry if telling you in such a direct way makes me look cheap to you. I don't want that. I'm human. I want. I need. I ache all over just wanting that intimacy I had for so many years. There are other things that are important, maybe even more important, but right now this is top priority. Believe me."

"What other things?"

"You know."

"Name them."

"The boys—your point. Religion—undecided. Finances—that's okay. Family—I don't even know how you feel about having a family."

"We already have one. I'd like more children, but I don't need more. Even?"

"Even."

"Then it sounds as if there's very little going against me, Bev. Just this one giant issue. Can't you have a little faith and wait?"

"No!"

"Well, why the hell not?"

"Because life has made me a realist. Sorry, Joe. I've been that 'faith and hope' route and I've been let down. I've been having a hard time dealing with the routine things I should be handling because I'm frustrated. I can't think clearly. I love and want you and you love and want me. I'm not suggesting anything horrible and wrong. I'm suggesting an intimate relationship between two people who love and want each other exclusively."

"Exclusively," he muttered. "That doesn't sound very committed."

"That's all I have right now. I don't want to make promises and deals. I just want to love you. Period."

"Are you really afraid it would be dull? You've had a little sample, baby. Do you think I couldn't be expressive enough? Ad-lib enough? Eager enough? Is that it?"

"Yes. I'm afraid of that."

"Maybe you're afraid I don't have enough experience. You've had a lot of experience."

"Well, after all, Joe, I was married for quite a few years. I know what I'm talking about."

"Think you can teach me something?"

"Now you're getting mad."

"Yes, I am dammit! You're already attacking my performance and you haven't even tried me yet. Let's go"

"Go where?"

"To bed. Come on, baby, show the dull, sanctimonious preacher how to screw. You're the expert!"

"Don't hurt me, Joe. Don't go in there mad."

"Too late. We're going to check it out, see if it works. I have to do it for you, right, Bev? Have to see if it's okay for you. I'm good enough to play with the kids, good enough to hold you and love you when you're down and scared and lonely. Let's see if good old Joe can pass the final exam. Now!"

Joe was getting pretty good at yelling too, Beverly thought. She followed him into the bedroom. She was scared silly. Her knees were wobbly and her hands were ice cold. Joe was yanking off his shoes angrily. Tearing off his shirt, pissed. Really fuming.

"Well, come on, Beverly, you're the expert. Do something. Strip."

"Stop it, Joe."

"No way, baby, there's no stopping it now. This is the big test. You win. I can't let you throw me out. I love you and if I want to stay with you, I have to really perform. Joe, the trained seal. Let's get it on. Let's see if old Joe is any good in bed."

"Forget it," she said quietly. "I want love, not war. It's over. We can't cross this gulch. Go home. Lock the door on your way out."

"No guts?"

"Fresh out. I don't want to force you into throwing away all your purity and virtue and then be the one to watch you crawl out of here and beg for forgiveness. I don't want to be your Eve, Joe. I wanted to love you."

"You know I wouldn't do that either. I'd never make you witness my sorrow or regrets. I wouldn't make you pay for anything I did. Why do you always pretend you don't know me when you know me better than anyone? Why, Bev? Open your damned eyes!"

That did it. How much hostility was a woman supposed to bear? And who was Joe mad at? Her? She went into the bathroom and locked the door. She didn't want to feel like a cheap whore for wanting the man she loved. She wouldn't come out, she told him, until she heard the door slam. So pretty soon she heard it... and she cried. Again.

Beverly took a shower. She just wanted to be clean before she killed herself. She wasn't about to spend another night alone in that big bed. Why is it that when you love a man he doesn't want to make love to you, and when you don't love a man that's all he wants? Well, maybe one more night, since she couldn't breathe enough water in the shower to drown herself.

Bev didn't want to come out of the bathroom and face an empty house, or her life, but she couldn't stay in the bathroom all night. She was just about ready to stop crying, but not quite. She sat down on the edge of the bed to finish her weeping, when she felt a foot. Some people threatened to wear out their welcome.

It was force of habit actually. Once you got used to falling into the assistant minister's arms every time you were crying, it became second nature. This was the first time he ever yanked off her towel and tossed it aside. She studied the face. The anger was gone. Joe couldn't stay mad for long.

"I'm sorry, Joe. I was wrong. I don't want you to do this. I know how you feel about it and I don't want to make you do something you'll regret. Especially on the threat that we're finished—I can't really give you up. I really do love you. So much. Even if you wouldn't blame me, we'd both know it was my fault. We just have a different point of view on this subject; maybe someday we'll work it out. I don't really want to stop seeing you."

"That's one thing about us preachers, Bev. When we decide to sin, we think of some very good reasons to justify it."

"What are your reasons?"

"Do you think I want you any less than another man in the same circumstances might want you? Do you think because my mind is bent to a certain path my body doesn't respond to love in a natural way? Do you think there is no limit to my restraint, my will? Oh, baby, I pray for strength all the time, but I keep loving and wanting you more, like any other man. I love you. I want you to be sure. That's the only real difference between us, Beverly. I'm already sure."

"Really, Joe? Look at me. Really look. This is how a woman over thirty looks after she's had children. A little saggy, a little stretched, and you might find something else a little stretched too. You should know, Joe. It might make a difference."

"Oh, yeah? Look what your saggy old body did to the preacher. I think I passed the first test."

"Oh, Joe." She sighed. "You're so beautiful. Firm and strong and young and beautiful. You should have a young virgin who is as lovely as you are."

"I'm old enough. And I've had a few young bodies. I'm looking for something more. I want you, Beverly. And I want you quiet for a change."

"Joe, I promise I won't be disappointed if it isn't terrific the very first time."

"That's a relief. It's gonna be lousy. I promise."

"You're sure."

"I'm sure I'm going to explode the minute I get inside you. This takes practice, you know."

"I know."

"Then if we've covered everything, could you shut up now?"

She could. For a change. For a while Beverly was very quiet because she was simply amazed with the way he took over. Joe had a light and thrilling touch and a knowledge of a woman's body that went far beyond her expectations.

She hadn't really thought it would be dull or boring. She had really thought it might be like this, because she knew Joe a lot better than she let on. And she hadn't thought he'd be disappointed in her slightly worn-out body. It was functional and what she lacked in newness she made up for with experience. Beverly wasn't ignorant of the thrust of a man's hips. She knew them well. And she responded well. Once you're accustomed to that sort of thing, you can let it happen, and if you love the man, it happens quickly. It happens to your body from a place inside your head that grows and builds and expands. And it is beautiful.

Bev was ready for Joe's urgency even before he warned her. She was prepared to help him even when he thought the last thing he needed was help. And he was right about that much. He exploded. But so did Beverly.

Just because you're a preacher doesn't mean you can't rejoice in that kind of pleasure. It doesn't mean you can't appreciate that kind of wild, mad intensity you brought to the woman you love. And the floating back is that much more glorious if you really love her. Softer, sweeter. And what a treat to learn that her cheeks really do flush just like in the dreams. Flushed and pink and fitting very appropriately on the face with the faint smile of success and fulfillment.

So now you have to ad-lib because you never had that experience before. You never had to pass your final exam before. For the first time in your life you brought the most magnificent pleasure created to a woman with whom you were wildly in love. So you kiss her whole body and don't let her jump up and run away because you want to touch her a little more. And you feel terrific and promise more of the same because, hell, who knew you were so good?

"Did you pray for that, Joe?"

"I wouldn't have dared."

"Are you sorry?"

"No, baby. Not sorry."

Joe held her close and touched her tenderly for a long time. He was filled with a contentment that his previous encounters with women had been lacking. Even though at this point in his life he doubted the great plan very little, he felt for the first time a profound knowledge of at least part of its purpose. While his body cried out that this was perfection, he was aware of what was missing to make this complete, whole. But the step had been taken, the line was crossed, and there was no retreat. He admitted his hunger and reached for her again.

Beverly yielded herself without thought because she knew this wasn't the kind of thing you could deny. It was the fact that when you thought you had it right you couldn't just lay back and appreciate your good luck, you had to test it to see if you had missed anything. You had to try to get better than perfect.

"Now, that had to be perfect, Beverly. Had to be."

"Pretty close."

"It gets better than that?"

Lots of sex made Beverly giggle just like lots of booze did. So she giggled. "I don't know, Joe. I can't say I've had better, but I don't want you to stop trying."

"Are we going to get any sleep?"

More giggling. Silly, stupid giggling. She didn't seem to be able to stop, so he asked her what was so damn funny.

"The sun's coming up, Joe. You have to go give a sermon."

"Beverly?"

"Huh?"

"Bev, I really want to hear you say that for about thirty years."

"Only thirty? Well, I guess even I could use some practice."

Joe looked at the clock. "It's only five-thirty."

"Forget it, Superman. I'm shot."

"I'm too tired to get up. You're bad, Beverly. Bad."

"You said I was good."

"You must be because I'm so tired. Let's go take a shower. Don't you have to get up and take a pill or something."

"Oh, God."

"Beverly, are you praying?"

"Yes."

"Oh, God!"

"Look, it's okay. I'm sure it's going to be okay. I'll take a look at the calendar, but I'm sure—"

"Beverly, what the hell happened? You were the one who insisted. You made the almighty decision. I thought you were prepared, safe. Bev?"

This was very embarrassing. She swallowed hard and faced him bravely. "Joe, I wasn't. Whatever you must think, I didn't plan what happened last night. All those things I said, well, I meant them, but I didn't plan it. I couldn't bear to see you walk out that door one more night. I never even thought about protection. I just... needed you... so bad."

"Well, what now, expert?"

"I have a prescription and I'll fill it. I'll take the pill. Now, I can't just start them, you know, I have to wait, and in the meantime you'll have to stop at the drugstore. Okay?"

"Awwww, Beverly!"

"Well, it's the only way, Joe."

"That is not an easy thing for a minister to do. What if one of the flock sees me buying rubbers or something?"

"Thank your lucky stars you don't have to wear a collar. Have you ever done that before? Stopped at the drugstore for a little protection?"

"Yep."

"The sin trip?"

"Even then I was a very careful sinner."

"That figures. Am I another sin trip?"

Beverly was apparently a little slow. "Beverly, when are you going to listen to me? I love you. I have loved you for a long time. I've wanted you forever. This is no small thing for me; this is not enough for me. Come on now, you're going to have to quit fooling around and think about this seriously for a change. I need a real commitment. I want to marry you and the boys and be with you all the time. I can't do this routine for very long. I'll give you a little time and I'll hope, but you hurry up. I need you."

It wasn't as though she hadn't already been thinking about it. She couldn't seem to think about anything else. When she prepared to marry Bob, there was no question in her mind. After a few years had passed she saw that much of what they had together was luck. Their love had been very committed; they managed to stick together long enough to solve their more serious problems. Who could predict a thing like stamina? In less fortunate unions the love had waned and faded. There was no great wealth of wisdom on her part that made her choice right. It just happened that they were well matched.

Thinking back realistically, even in their good marriage there had been some blistering quarrels. They suffered through petty squabbles about money and chores and other things. Even sex. After Bob's death Bev realized how much she depended on him, and his memory became more perfect with every passing day. Theirs had been one of the better marriages on record, even with all its flaws.

In church that morning she took an aisle seat so she could get a good view of the preacher. She watched him with love and longing in her eyes. She noted the bright smile, the commanding manner. His flock loved him, needed him. He led them gently, sincerely. This was his calling. She never doubted his faith, but it wasn't faith alone that put him on a pulpit, or moved God to put him there, if you believed all that stuff. He was a magnificent speaker. He had imagination, a creative ability to make his message moving, believable, interesting, and fun. And he was so terrific with people, large groups or individuals with secret problems or despairs. The perfect preacher. She figured he was about one in a million.

Joe didn't seem to lean toward ambition, except maybe within himself, but she could see that he could have great success in the ministry. Beliefs aside, he had that national television charisma, that perfect mixture of innocence and mastery.

She looked around the congregation. They needed him. They depended on his words, his faith, his judgment, and his knowledge. He would leave Maple Hills and move to another church. A church of his own. There would be a trusting congregation, a modest parsonage—and a faithful wife? Oh, she loved him, loved him desperately. But if they married, what would his flock think of a wife who wasn't even sure she believed in God? Joe didn't seem to be very distressed about that now, but that could change. Would she have to pretend? Would his followers question his sincerity if he were to marry someone like her?

Beverly didn't always sense disaster when she looked ahead. Once she had been optimistic and self-assured. But now she was simply scared silly. What if her marriage to Joe would hurt his career? What if his career hurt their marriage? And worse, she thought as she looked lovingly, longingly, at the man in the pulpit, what if he died? How could she collect the insurance money, give away his clothes, and explain to the boys that they had to make it without a father... again?

Oh, God, could I live through any more grief? Dear Lord, it would hurt to see him go. Would it hurt more to need him, build a life with him, and then lose him?

Or God, what if he suffered because of me? Could I watch the disappointment in his eyes as he tried to live faithfully with his mistake? Dear God, if you can't save me, please save him. He is too valuable to waste. Oh, God, is anything forever? Is anything for sure?

Just about one thing, Bev. Just about one thing is forever, for sure. Think about it.

I didn't hear that. I hang around this place too much. It's making me punchy.

"I wonder, Reverend, are you free to come to Sunday dinner?"

"In a flash."

"Joe, we need to talk."

That was all he needed to hear to know that something very heavy lay ahead. He rushed to her door, half afraid of what she had on her mind. When he walked in, he was all set to have it out with her. "What's the matter?"

"I'm happy, Joe. Thanks."

"Great. What's wrong?"

"I feel guilty. About last night."

"I don't. I love you too much to feel bad about loving you."

"You're good, Joe. Too good to be led into a bad—"

"Bev, stop," he said, reaching for her. "I was not led. I did what I did of my own free will. No one is responsible for my actions but me."

"Will you wait for me, Joe? For a little while? I'll be faithful to you. I have so many doubts and fears. I have to settle them first and you can't really help me. I'm not stalling; I'm really scared. Before I marry you, I want to be sure I can be a good wife to you. For your sake, let me be sure."

"I have given you everything I have to give, Beverly. I don't have anything more. And I'm starting to have needs too. I don't know what you're waiting for."

"Aside from all my other doubts, I don't know how I could be a preacher's wife if I don't even believe in God. That's the big one. You must understand that?"

"I understand a lot more than you give me credit for. I'd like you to find faith in God, not for me, not for Him. For yourself. I know that's a tough one to resolve." He hung his head and could not look at her, as if he had trouble with the words. Joe and words were almost synonymous. He never struggled for the right thing to say. "I think we could make it fine, though, if you had a little faith in me."

"Oh, Joe..."

"Just love me. For right now, while you're thinking, just love me."

Twelve

ev was letting the time roll by. She took on the added obligation of teaching a summer charm course to thirteen- year-old girls. Mothers panicked when their daughters reached that age. They were usually one extreme or the other: clumsy and gawky or real little sexpots. Bev suspected the girls would be fine without charm, but their mothers might not, so she tried to help mold them into young women.

There was still extra time. She spent it looking for an apartment for Steve and Terry. She decided they were spending too much money to be near the campus and thought they would do better on the other side of town, on a bus route. Beverly was keeping busy.

She had looked at the calendar on that very important day in May. She wasn't very pleased with what she saw. After a short lecture to herself on lousing things up, she vowed not to think about it until it was necessary. She was the all-time worrywart too. Worry could make you two or three weeks late.

Joe took a look at the calendar too. It hung on the inside of the kitchen cupboard door so it wasn't too hard to peek without Beverly knowing. Women had to keep track of things so they could be prepared. Beverly didn't know Joe looked. She expected him to pray while she kept busy to keep from worrying.

Now, Beverly was subtle, but if you knew what you were looking for, it wasn't very hard to break the code. There was a little pencil line through the date on the calendar every four weeks. Every fourth Friday exactly since January on that calendar. Joe suspected that if he could get his hands on some old calendars, he would see years of those subtle little pencil lines. She ticked like a regular clock.

There should have been a big red star on the Saturday just two weeks after the last pencil line.

For once Beverly kept her mouth shut and, as usual, Joe didn't say anything. He stopped at the drugstore. Every time he went into the kitchen he checked to see if a pencil line had appeared on the calendar.

Maple Hills and Beverly were separated by a few miles, so it wasn't very likely that a parishioner would see Joe's car at Beverly's house in the late, late night. And the approach of summer would mean getting to know the neighbors, which Joe and Bev did, neglecting to mention Joe's profession.

Summertime also meant T-ball for Mark. Joe practiced with him and took Chuck and Bev to the games. He was growing more like a father to them all the time. They were close to Joe and trusted him. There were problems that arose when kids started getting popular with peers. Things had to be gone over and discussed. With little boys, sometimes it had to be with a man. And Joe was very good at that too.

Joe spent so much time at Beverly's house that it had become an established courtship as far as the rest of the world was concerned. This Saturday was no exception. Mark wanted to go swimming. It was the first week in June and the community pool had opened.

"I don't know, Mark. It's still a little cool. Maybe Joe and I will take you next weekend."

"Maaaa, jeeez, all the other kids are going."

"Sorry. Anyway, you were supposed to clean your room. Is it done?"

"I ain't gonna do it! Chuck always messes it up anyway. You don't never make him do nothin'!"

"Mark!" The voice of Joe, low and firm. Joe was fixing the screen door like a good weekend husband and father.

"Awwww, get off my back!"

Beverly didn't think she had ever seen a man move that fast. Not even when trying to make a home run out of a two-base hit. Joe could really move. Mark couldn't move nearly fast enough because he got it, right on the seat on his pants. It made a very loud thwack, followed by an unhappy and surprised yelp. There was momentary silence as the twosome entered the bedroom in question. A few minutes later Joe came out alone.

"I don't know if I should let you do that," she said.

"Let? Was I supposed to ask? I didn't have time."

"What did you say to him?"

"We had a very short discussion. We'll talk later when he's had time to calm down. He's mad now."

"Well, tell me, Joe. He's my son."

"He said, 'You can't spank me, you ain't my dad,' and I said, 'I know who I am; now, clean up this room,' and he said, 'Why should I?' and I said, 'Because if you don't, you're going to get another spanking,' and he pouted and I said, 'We'll talk about your mouth when the room is clean,' and he said, 'Okay.'"

"Well, I don't know, Joe. They like you so much. It might be a bad idea to have you start disciplining them. Maybe you ought to just leave that to me."

"Mmm."

"Mmm?"

"Well, Beverly, I just did it because I don't want Mark to talk like that, to you or to anyone else. When I'm not here and he talks to you that way, you handle it your way. But I'm here a lot, and when he talks to me that way, he's going to deal with it on my terms. My terms are these—first I get your attention, then later we have a civilized discussion. Next time, you run it through your brain once before you send it out your mouth. Or else."

"Well—"

"Why don't you just wait and see?"

The room got cleaned. Best job ever. Not only that, but Mark was sorry and polite and sweet. Joe had this habit of making himself seem irresistible. Mark needed a father. He needed Joe. Beverly's reluctance was starting to mess things up for the boys.

Joe was a regular on Saturday nights. There was seldom any church business and he had a standing invitation to dinner. So they finished dinner and the dishes and settled into what looked like an all-American family setting. The boys were in front of the TV, Bev was on the couch paging through a magazine, and Joe was working on a bank statement at the dining room table. That's when the phone rang. Bev picked it up innocently.

"Hey, beautiful. How're you?"

"John? Is that you?"

"It's me, beautiful. How's my big sister?"

"John, are you drunk?"

"Very, very drunky. Very. Is your lover boy there?"

"Joe? Yes, Joe is here."

"Well, then let me talk to him, sweetheart. I've got a good deal for him. Now, hurry up, angel, I have to pee.

Bev didn't have to call Joe to the phone. The worried and surprised look on her face said it all.

"John? Hey, buddy, what's up?"

"Your big opportunity, pal," John said, adding a sniff and a gurgle. "Your big chance to get some points with the Chief. I'm at Tarran's Tavern on Seventieth and Cash. If you hurry up, you can save my life."

"Need a ride home, John?"

"Hey, Joe, I'm giving you the big chance here, pal. If you can give me one reason to go on with this farce, I won't throw my ass over the Cash Street Bridge. Okay?"

"Okay. Sit tight. I'm on my way."

Joe was a little surprised that Bev didn't slow him down by questions as he shot out the door. He said quickly that he had to get to John before he tried to drive himself anywhere. He was also amazed that she believed him when he said he probably wouldn't be back after driving John home because it would take him so long. He told her he would see her in the morning.

Joe had a pain that told him that if this was real trouble and he was too late, he would be a long time getting over it. He pulled into Tarran's, one of the sleaziest bars he'd seen in a long time. He relaxed when he saw John, far to the rear of the bar, with his head down on the table. Joe hoped he had passed out, but no such luck.

Joe wanted to take him right out of there and find a nice place to sober up and talk, but the minute he pulled on John's arm he said, "Not so fast, Preacher." It was like calling "Fire!" The place started to thin.

Joe didn't ask why John was on a binge, but John was more than ready to spill. Joe wasn't going to be able to do John any good in this place, in this condition, but he was sort of getting the story. It apparently hadn't happened all at once, which it almost never does, but it had come to the boiling point early that morning. John didn't want to handle life anymore.

First, the nurse dumped him. Well, that was no big deal except that John loved her. Really loved her and wanted to marry her. But she wanted to marry a specialist. She'd been fooling around with a specialist, for God's sake, the whole time.

And the hospital couldn't share him with the clinic in which he was moonlighting. He needed the money so badly, sometimes he took something to stay awake and keep him going. Nothing really illegal, but a little something. Then he received a warning: quit the extra job, or out you go. Just like that, after about eight years of work.

Then, a few months ago, one of John's closest friends was suspended because a young male patient—a boy of twelve—brought charges against him for sexual assault. It was nonsense. But it mushroomed, made the papers, criminal charges were filed, it was going to court. John stood by him; he didn't even think the guy was gay, and even if he was gay, he'd never hurt a kid. He just knew the guy wasn't a sex offender. Wouldn't John know a thing like that after eight years of working with him?

No, he didn't. His friend had broken under the pressure and admitted his guilt. His lifetime career dreams were over, so he shot himself. In the head. They had found him this morning. And he left a note. He was sorry.

John had had it. He didn't want to live in a crazy, screwed-up world like this. But John was too drunk to throw himself over anything, especially a bridge. He couldn't do anything but go with Joe. Joe thought his own apartment would be the best place to exorcise the demons from a bad drunk. It wasn't going to be fun.

John cried and puked and shook. Joe held his head like he would a sick child and mopped up a lot. It was a long time before John slept, and even then it was troubled, exhausted sleep. It wasn't as if Joe hadn't seen this before. Once this was Joe. But when it happened to him there was no one to hold his head, mop up, and love him like a brother.

Joe waited until the sun came up to call Charles Sullivan, the chief reverend.

"Charles? Did I wake you? I know it's early."

"No, I was up. What can I do for you?"

"Well, if you've got a spare sermon laying around, you can do the early service for me. I have an urgent pastoral duty sleeping off a bad drunk in my bed."

"One of the flock?"

"Yep."

"Can I help?"

"I can handle it, Charles. He came to me, so I think he'll be all right. But he was doing some pretty wild talking last night and I don't want to leave him alone until I'm sure."

"Sure. Call me later and let me know."

"Will do. Oh, and Charles. Bev will be there and she may ask you where I am. Tell her I called you, okay, and tell her I was called out this morning. I really don't want her to come over here, but if you tell her I turned my apartment into a drunk tank, she'll come. Don't give her the details, okay?"

"Sure." Charles would know after the early service who was in trouble. Steve and Terry would probably be in church. And Charles, like many people, knew Beverly the nosy.

It was noon before John began to come out of it. The first sounds from the bed sent Joe for the pail again. The next sounds were a multitude of apologies and excuses. Sober, John was going to pretend it wasn't all that bad. Just the booze. Joe wasn't buying.

"I'm sure it was the booze, which is one of many things we'll have to discuss. But I'll take the sober version anyway."

The sober version was no different. John didn't want to tell it because telling it, hearing it come out of his own mouth, made it too real. It made him cry some more.

"Where do you think you had the first problem?" Joe asked.

"I don't know. They stacked up pretty fast."

"Janet? Your friend's suicide? The extra job? The pills? The liquor?"

"Maybe Janet."

"Did you take pills while you were with Janet?"

John looked at Joe directly. His eyes were red-rimmed, blank, exhausted, naked. "Yes." Then he slumped, visibly, into utter disappointment. "And that guy, my friend, the closet sex offender, he let me help him. He swore he was innocent and lied to me, laying my own credibility on the line. And I'm about to lose my license before I get it."

"You're lucky."

"Yeah, lucky."

"Yeah, real lucky. All you have to do is quit the job. You could have gotten a worse ultimatum; they could have told you to go into drug treatment or hit the trail."

John hung his head. "I didn't do a lot of that."

"What do you want, John? Next?"

"I need some rest. Breakfast and maybe a day off."

"And then?"

"I'll be all right. I can handle it."

"Yeah, I saw."

"That won't happen again, Joe. Don't worry."

Joe grabbed his upper arm. "You don't puke all over my apartment and then tell me you're okay. If you hadn't been so damn drunk, you might have had the strength to hurt yourself. You said you wanted to die. You said it ten or a hundred times."

"I did. Last night I did. I'm okay now."

"Next time you might not accidentally get smashed and be too drunk to shoot yourself. Next time you want to die, you might be sober."

"I can handle it myself. Alone."

"Which is how all this started. No, it wasn't Janet, or the extra job, or the guy that betrayed you. Listen here, I'm not going to strap myself to you and watch over you. But I'm telling you straight up you have two choices as I see it. You can work this whole business through with some professional help, or you can wait for the next time things stack up and hope you get through it. Which?"

"I want things to be all right. I want everything to be all right again."

"Hey, John. It just plain never is. Never! You can either learn how to live it through, or let it kill you."

John sniveled again. Then he began some full-fledged crying. "Is there anything in this whole stupid world that is just all right? For sure? Certain?"

Joe put his arms around John and held him, rubbing his back while he cried. "Yeah. About one thing. I'll tell you about it sometime. First, let's go out and get breakfast."

There were a few things that needed adjustment right away. Rest, money, good food, no chemicals, and some self-esteem. It is very embarrassing for a man who is studying in a field as complicated as medicine to admit to such a vulnerability, such a problem with his own sense of reason. But when the preacher can confess even worse loss of perspective, it helps. They set up a schedule to get together every day until John found the counselor of his choice. And there would be plenty of time to solve all the problems. Taking one small problem at a time would be a good place to start. "Don't try to settle everything today. You have enough headaches to spread out over the year."

"Friend, I have a headache you could never relate to."

"Don't count on it, John."

Joe went to Beverly later that afternoon. She met him at the door with, "What's the matter with John?" Beverly didn't waste any time.

"After the boys have gone to bed, honey," Joe said.

"He was really blasted," he told her later. "He was so sick I didn't want to leave him. He really tied one on."

"What else?"

"Else?"

"I have a right to know. He's my brother."

"Of course. Well, everything in the world has crashed down on John. The hospital found out he was moonlighting and they're forcing him to quit. He had a big blowout with Janet, who has not been entirely faithful, and they're quits. And a friend of his, the guy you probably read about, accused of molesting a kid, admitted it and killed himself. He was a friend of John's."

"Whew. Who'd have guessed?"

"John did the sensible thing and got smashed. But he's going to be all right."

"You told me. You went right ahead and told me!"

"He gave me permission, Beverly. Don't get excited. I'm not breaking any more oaths for you."

"Does he need money? I have money."

"We know, Beverly. He needs space and time and he knows where the bank is."

"Okay."

"Beverly, you're getting smarter."

Beverly was also getting lovelier. By the day, the hour, and the minute. She was blooming. Joe knew it was their intimate relationship that was responsible. She wasn't alone in that big bed anymore. Joe would stay with her until the early hours of the morning, and she was resting. He was aware that she reached for him in her sleep, sighed when she touched him, and found contentment and security in his presence. She was happier and wilier. She was enticing, charming, letting him lead sometimes, trying to please him, submitting to his will like a compliant mistress. Very attractive.

"Come here, beautiful, and love me."

"I do love you, Joe."

"Then check on the boys and see if they're asleep."

"For someone who wanted to wait, you sure can't get enough."

"I stopped at the drugstore and this thing is burning a hole in my pocket."

"Why don't you buy a carton of those things?"

"Why don't you?"

"I did. I put them in the drawer by the bed. Your side."

"Beverly, you're nuts."

No, she wasn't. She did buy them and they were there, on the side that had become his. She was trying to help him out if she could.

For nearly two weeks Joe saw John every day. Rest from giving up the extra job, no more uppers, and someone who cared showed on him right away. He figured he could manage on what little bit of money he had, and he found a good therapist right at the hospital who was eager to straighten him out. He was on his way to dealing with life.

The month of June was wearing old. Joe was seeing less of John but heard improvement in his voice, and knew he was getting consistently better, stronger. Joe was still looking for that subtle pencil mark and stopping at the drugstore, but less frequently on the latter.

Joe received his notice. He was getting his own church. He would be assigned to a small church in California. The Santa Monita Christian Church. He wouldn't be the assistant, he would be the head honcho, the chief reverend. They would have a nice parsonage for him and his family, if he could get one. He had to be there by August thirty-first.

And in came July. Rushing him. Pushing and shoving him. He didn't want to see what he was seeing and if he could close his eyes to it he would. Beverly was back to crying more often. She was growing buxom and tender and while she wanted Joe beside her at night, she wasn't exactly amorous. She was hard on the boys and impatient with Joe. And she thought dumb old Joe didn't guess what was going on.

It wasn't a habit of Joe's to go to the church alone in the evening to pray, although he loved what the sinking sun did to a stained glass window. Now he developed the habit. He was comfortable there. There was something about a church, the way it was prayed for, maintained by the faithful that made him proud. A place for them to come for peace and stability. For something that could endure.

Now, after many years and some confusion, he would get his own church. It was what he had wanted, to help the living with his work. He would have responsibility for a trusting congregation. A dream come true, or so he had thought.

He looked up at the cross that hung over the altar. His hands were plunged deeply into his pockets and he stared at the symbol that drove him. Doubt, he thought. The big "D."

Ever since he was a kid, Joe's sins had been the real obvious kind. The first time he lied, he was caught. The only time he ever lifted a candy bar from the corner drugstore, he got nabbed. Joe couldn't get away with anything.

So he prayed... again.

Oh, I didn't come here to ask You. I already know what I have to do. I just wanted to tell You again that I'm sorry it had to be this way. I had it planned all different. I never meant to hang so many lives in the balance. My fault, of course. Well, the commitment didn't start with the baby. It started a long time ago, way back when I didn't want Beverly to be lonely anymore.

Now it's time, and I don't know if I can replace Bob. I don't want to, but that's what she doesn't seem to understand. I don't expect her to forget him, stop missing him, stop loving him, stop seeing him in her sons. I just want to be next, after him. And I want her to find some peace. So maybe she needs me more than Santa Monita does. I don't have a choice anymore. Don't take it too hard. I couldn't have left her even if she hadn't gotten pregnant. And please... don't be too upset with Bev. She can't help it. She's just so scared.

If it's all right with You, I'm not going to mail that resignation right away. I'm going to wait a little longer and pray a little harder. Oh, Lord, I am so selfish. I still want it all. But I'll take it on the chin. Anyway You say.

You know what I'm going to do. Do You want me to see that's how it all started? I'm not really blind. I know where I went wrong. But the only thing I can do is love her. The only thing I can give her to make her happy is wrong. How did You ever get

Yourself mixed up with a guy like me? Lord, I am unworthy. But I'll go to her again, even without her commitment to me, and let myself in with my own key and love her and hold her, and You will have seen me fail again. By now it must be a pretty common sight. But I'll take any help available. A little push in the right direction, maybe? I could try to make it up to You. I'd like a chance.

Oh, and about that baby. I'd like a girl. Amen.

It wasn't exactly a divine answer. More a lack of alternatives. Joe wondered if that was the same thing as an answer from heaven. He finished up the paperwork that had accumulated on his desk early in the day. Then he called John and asked for some time.

John could give him a few minutes if he could make it fast. So how do you rush a thing like this? It was enough to make a guy sick.

"I have a problem... personal... a very personal problem. I... ah, I could use a friend and some advice."

"How the tables turn," was the first thing John said. "I ought to beat the hell out of you," was the next thing he said. Finally, he said, "Okay, I'll do whatever I can."

Thirteen

Beverly's days had not been starting out very well. But this morning she felt a little better because at least she had some plans.

She knew what Carl was going to do, what he was going to say, and how she was going to react afterward. It was just a formality. She already knew she was pregnant. She had known it for a long time.

She thought when she first looked at the calendar that probably she was pregnant because she was a lot of things, but mostly she was fertile. When she was forty-eight hours late she was sure. When her bra started feeling tight, she was even more sure. When she threw up, she was almost suicidal.

She pulled on the once nice-fitting summer slacks and sleeveless blouse with a deep sigh; everything felt tight. She headed out the door. She had the little bottle in her purse, another ridiculous formality, and was on her way to Carl, the friendly neighborhood ob-gyn.

She did what any other neurotic, slightly off balance, unmarried pregnant woman would do when she saw her doctor walk into the office to greet her. She just about took his head off.

"Okay, Dr. Panstiel, let's see if just this once you can act like a professional and do the damned exam, give me the verdict, and let me out of here without any lip."

"Nice to see you too, Beverly."

"Oh, shut up!"

Carl looked at the chart to see if he could determine the cause of his favorite patient's unusually foul temper. "Pregnancy examination and prenatal check." As he stood there gawking at her chart, she glided past him into the examining room to strip, just like always. This time, though, she wasn't going to get all bleary-eyed and sloppy. She was almost thirty-five, dammit, and a little too old to have to get married.

She was apparently too old to have any secrets either. Carl knew Joe and Joe was a minister and her life now would be an open book. So why didn't she go to another doctor? That, she hadn't even considered. Carl was her doctor. Carl's office had her chart. And maybe Carl could get through to her, but she doubted it because she was mad. Really mad.

She didn't start out mad. She started out confused and scared. She even tried to pray about it and then got mad because all she could feel was nausea. It was time for action and not to mope around with the uncomfortable combination of cold dread and blind faith.

Life is different when you're almost thirty-five, widowed, and pregnant. There is a little less reason for hope when you've lived through a tragedy. You know how much it can hurt you, your kids, and other people when you make big mistakes. Ministers are included in the people group. Sometimes you just had to use good sense and try not to get too emotional.

Sure, Joe thought marriage was the answer to everything, but when had he been married? And when had he ever learned first-hand how horrible it could be to try to get through a failed relationship? And he would love having a baby, but what did he know about having a baby? He hadn't ever lived with a pregnant woman. He hadn't ever had to lift the diaper pail out of the tub to take a shower... every time he wanted to take a shower. He didn't understand postpartum blues or breastfeeding. Oh, he would be thrilled about having a baby, because he didn't have a clue what it was like. No, Joe could stick to saving souls and Beverly would handle the real-life stuff. Beverly the wise, strong, sensible, logical.

"Okay, Mrs. Simpson, all done. If you will dress and step into my office, I will discuss my findings with you." Dr. Panstiel, the professional.

"Yes, Doctor." Beverly the polite.

Carl was going to get to her, make her mad, she could feel it. He wouldn't have to try very hard. She had been looking for a good fight and there was no one else with whom to fight. Carl drew the short straw when he entered ob. He wouldn't have nearly as many mental cases in psychiatry. That's the way it goes, Carl baby. Here I come.

"Sit down and cool off, Beverly. I don't want to fight."

"When did you get to know me so well?"

"Well, you're looking for a fight, aren't you? Go ahead, deny it."

"So I told you I get crabby—"

"On the pill. You told me you got crabby on the pill. You obviously have not been taking your pills."

"What was your first clue?"

"What are you going to do?"

"None of your business."

"That's a good girl, just let it all out."

"Carl, I'm warning you—"

"Does Joe know?"

"Know what? I don't even know. Am I?"

"You knew you were pregnant when you made the appointment. Did you tell him?"

"No. And you better not either, Carl. Doctor-patient relationship and all that."

"Now, that's a hell of a thing to stick me with, Beverly. You know how I care about you and Joe. Talk to me, please."

"There's nothing to talk about."

"Bull."

"Don't get tough with me, Carl, or I'll scream rape."

"You're already dressed."

"Carl!"

"Okay, okay, now what are you going to do?"

"Well, I already threw up and I suppose you want to know if I need anything for my bowels and there will be the usual vitamins and—"

"Beverly, goddammit—"

"Carl, I don't know. I think I know, but I'm not sure. I only just found out. Don't badger me, Carl. I have to think."

"What if I tell him?"

"You won't."

"How do you know?"

"Because if you do, I'm going to sue you right out of your boxer shorts, that's how I know. And I mean it."

"Then why did you come to me when you knew what I was going to say and how I would worry about you and everything? Why didn't you go to some other doctor and keep it from me; some doctor who doesn't care about you and the baby's father so much?"

Beverly had the good grace to let one tear collect and run slowly down her cheek, quite a long way down before she brushed it off. It was more dramatic if you did that. "Because, Carl. You're my doctor."

"You have to tell Joe."

"Is that your professional opinion?"

"Yes."

"Well, I'll think about it. Thank you, Doctor. Good day."

"Good day, my ass."

Mrs. Simpson waltzed out of the office and Carl couldn't move. He supposed it wouldn't be right to call Joe, even though he knew Beverly wouldn't really sue him. Would she? She was usually sensible. Sometimes. But it wasn't his place to interfere. For lack of a better answer, Carl clasped his hands together in front of his face and looked at the ceiling in his little cubicle. "A few dates, a nice wedding, so what was I asking? Didn't You build any restraint into that model? I can't do anything. I hope You've got some ideas. And hurry. Amen."

There was a knock at the door and he remembered that he had another patient in another examining room, waiting with her feet up in the air while the vent cooled her bottom. He said, "Come in."

"Did Mrs. Simpson leave her medical records in here, Doctor?"

"Didn't she drop them at the desk as usual?"

"She must have inadvertently taken them with her. If she doesn't bring them right back, I'll call her later and remind her to return them."

Inadvertently, my aunt Sarah.

"Mrs. Williamson is ready in Room Four."

"Thank you," he said. He still couldn't move. "Faster," he said to the ceiling. "Amen."

Beverly went directly to the hospital. She was in a hurry and called ahead to John to say she was coming to see him about an urgent family matter. There was simply no one else in whom she could confide. She needed some help. She needed someone she could trust. Terry would try, but would get upset. There was almost nothing worse than an upset bride. And Terry was so very young. John was a doctor. He was rational and strong. He would be objective.

John met her in the lobby, telling her he had borrowed an empty office from a nursing instructor on the fifth floor. It would be his for up to four hours. Beverly stopped short when she saw that the office came with a secretary in an outer office, but John urged her on and closed the door.

"What's the problem?"

"I hardly know where to start. How about I'm pregnant?"

"That's a good start. How the hell did that happen?"

"Really, John, and you a doctor and everything."

"Beverly, come on!"

"I wasn't prepared. Now, what I have to know is how to go about having an abortion, a nice safe one, not in a clinic, out of town maybe, without anyone—"

"Abortion? Beverly, are you crazy?"

"Will you lower your voice, please."

"Are you out of your mind?"

"Simmer down. Really, John, I thought I could count on you to stay cool. I should have gone to Terry."

"You should have gone to Joe."

"Then you're certain the baby is Joe's?"

"Knock it off, Beverly!"

"For some reason I really wanted to try that out. Well, listen, I know perfectly well that Joe loves me and would like to marry me. But I do not want to get married right now, and I especially don't want to marry someone because I'm pregnant. I don't want anyone to know because I don't want any trouble."

"You are out of your mind."

"Well, that may be, but my mind is made up just the same."

"And Joe has nothing to say about this?"

"Oh, sure, I should tell him and hear his side of the story. Do you think that's likely to do me any good? I already told you, he'll want to get married and have the baby, and that's not what I want to do. Joe is an idealist. He goes around believing everything will be all right all the time. Now, can you see me, the preacher's wife, pouring tea at the church socials? Joe doesn't need a wife who doesn't even believe it's real. He could go so far, John. I'm only going to slow him down, hold him back. And what would his nice little congregation think of the reason we got married?"

"Who's going to tell?"

"That sort of thing tends to get out. I'm not right for Joe. Not now, anyway. And I would be as miserable as he would, trying to be something I thought I should be... oh, John, I just can't handle all that now. Not yet. Maybe later, when I'm ready, if he still wants me. But now, this is the only way."

"Beverly, I am sure that you are a very screwed-up woman."

"Are you going to help me or should I go somewhere else? There are plenty of clinics."

"What do you want me to do?"

"Well, help me get to the right doctor, in a hospital. You never know how uninformed you are about a thing like this until you're in trouble. Well, John?"

"Yes, Beverly, I'm going to help you."

"Whew. I hoped you would."

"It just so happens that I have a friend who handles little things like this all the time. You won't even know you've done it."

"Perfect."

"Let me go see if I can get him on the phone. Want to go out for coffee, or wait here?"

"I'll just wait here."

"All right, sit tight."

John used the secretary's phone. Reverend Clark was not in the church office, but they thought he could be found at the gym. John asked the secretary to place the call, track him down, tell him it was urgent, and then put the call through to John in the inner office. She was not to say that it was Reverend Clark on the line, because the woman he was with was very disturbed and might bolt. He felt marvelously smart and sneaky. John the double agent.

The secretary had a coffeepot in her part of the office and John poured two cups, not knowing how long it might take to find Joe. He caught Beverly sniffing and it made him feel extremely good.

"What's the matter with you? Didn't I fix it for you?" Just because you felt good didn't mean you had to be nice.

"Simply because I know what I have to do doesn't make it easy, John. I don't know if I'll ever be the same."

"Then put it off, Bev."

"How long can you put off something like this? I'm about out of time."

"I think you should talk to Joe. Give him a chance."

"No, not this time. Ministers can't help when they're emotionally involved. He would get sloppy and beg."

"Joe? Get sloppy? I don't think so."

"John, forget it."

"Well, you're not going to get any abortion today. It takes a few days. Why don't I go home with you and take the boys to the pool for the rest of the afternoon? You can take a nap and think this over."

"That would be nice, John. Thanks."

John tried to hide his wicked smile when he heard the buzzer on the phone. He knew Joe would understand his deceptive conversation, and, still pretending to talk to his doctor friend, that he could concoct a plan of action without Beverly guessing a thing. Shouldn't betrayal feel a little sickening? It didn't. Not a bit.

"Hiya, buddy, how are you? Good. Good. Yeah, I need a favor. It's my sister. She's pregnant and she'd like me to help her set up an abortion out of town. Yeah, yeah, I know, but you know how these things are, sometimes it just seems like the best thing to do. So, I told her I have a friend who handles things like this—No, no, her mind is definitely made up, but I'll ask her if you want me to... except that she'll probably only cry some more. Yeah, that's what I think too. Well, listen, I'm going to be out of the hospital the rest of the day. I'm going home with her and am taking her kids to the pool for the afternoon so she can take a breather. How about if I get back to you later and see if you came up with anything. Yeah, that sounds perfect. Great, great, that'll be good. So we're even? Good. Oh, and I really appreciate this. See ya."

"Will he take care of me, John?"

"Oh, yes, Beverly. Come on, let's get you home so you can take a nap or something."

"That sounds good."

"Where's Joe today?"

"He's all tied up, why?"

"You're not planning to see him?"

"Not until late tonight. He has meetings."

"Do you really think you're pulling this off without him knowing?"

"How would he know?"

"You don't think he might guess?"

She shrugged. "He doesn't know much about women."

"He knows enough. You're pregnant."

"That was my fault, John. Joe is a victim of circumstances."

"Oh? And what are you?"

"Dumb. Just plain dumb."

Fourteen

J ohn had the boys in Beverly's car. He wouldn't get wet
with them today, but he would take them out for a
hamburger later so they brought along a change of
clothes. He told her to calm down, get some rest, and think things
through again. It wasn't too late to change her mind.

Chuck was hollering for Uncle John to hurry up, but John
lingered. He really did love Beverly; he wasn't confused about
that. He simply couldn't let her go on with this. Oh, if she was
really in a jam and needed an abortion, he might help her with
that. But this was different. She might never trust him again. She
might hate him for a while. He hoped that someday she would
thank him.

But not right now. Right now she was staring with wide,
horrified eyes at the brown station wagon that was screaming up
the street toward the house. She was too stunned to speak until
she saw Joe jump out of the car and head toward her. He was
wearing only jogging shorts and shoes, a towel around his neck,
no shirt. He came from the gym on an urgent pastoral duty.
Beverly.

"You sold me out," she said to John.

"Yep," he said, sprinting off toward her car with her keys in
his hand.

Beverly wasn't having any of it. She whirled, ran into the
house, slammed the door, and locked it. John watched for a
minute. He kind of hated to miss this. Joe didn't look the least bit
reasonable. He looked pretty steamed. But he had his own key.
Foiled again, Beverly.

"Abortion?"

"Now, Joe, be reasonable—"

"Reasonable! This time you've gone too far, lady, too far!"

"I've done a lot of thinking, Joe, and it would be for the best if—"

"Just be quiet for once, and I really mean it. What can be going on in that head of yours? Are you crazy? That's my baby you want to kill. Mine! Don't you have any sense of decency?"

"I didn't want—"

"That's exactly what you wanted to do. Exactly. And I won't let you. I don't care what I have to do. I won't let you do it."

"Joe, listen to me. It can't work out the way you want it too. I wish it could, but it can't. It won't."

"Why?"

"I can't be a minister's wife."

"Why?"

"You know why. Because I wouldn't do you honor, you wouldn't be proud of me. People should respect a minister's wife and they would wonder where in the world you'd found me. You know yourself that I'm not even sure I believe in God."

"Well, I'm very sorry about that, Beverly, and I'll help you with that as much as you want, but that is not the issue here. The issue is the baby, and it's mine, and I want it even if you don't."

"But I don't want to get married!"

"Well, I'm sorry about that, too, because we're a little short on alternatives."

"What do you mean?"

"I made that baby, Beverly, and I can't make you marry me, but I won't let you get rid of it. I'll stay right here, night and day, and I won't leave. It's mine too!"

"Calm down. Jeez, it's not that dramatic. It was an accident, Joe. We were just fooling around and had an—"

"You were just fooling around maybe, not me! That's the difference between us, baby. You can ignore life's obligations if they get to be a little tough. Did you really think I set aside everything I believe in, everything I am, when I crawled in here late at night to make love to you? Maybe you thought I left it on your doorstep and then picked everything up when I was sneaking out before the sun came up. You can do that, maybe. Not me. I'm stuck with what I am and I have to live with myself."

"Ignore life's obligations? You bastard! How can you say that to me? Here is my little fatherless family, Mommy bearing all the responsibilities alone, the whole damn mess alone, and I try to spare you and—"

"Alone! Quit acting like a child, dammit, and grow up. Alone!"

Joe's face was very red. He slammed his fist into the palm of his other hand. She suspected he really did want to belt her.

"You haven't been alone. Who's been cutting the damn grass, going to the damn T-ball games, tightening all the loose screws around here? If I could only get my hands on that loose screw in your head. Beverly, I've been here for months. Months! What the hell do I have to do?"

"You're really making me sorry I taught you how to yell."

"Well, you've taught me a few things, but that wasn't one of them."

"Stop yelling. I want to talk. Like we used to."

"I don't know if I can." He sat on the sofa and put his head in his hands. Then he was on his feet again, in the kitchen, rummaging through the cupboards. "Where is the booze?"

"I don't have any."

"When did you stop having any?"

"I don't know."

"Well, when are you going to clean those cupboards. They're a mess. Everything is a mess! You're a mess!"

"Oh, stop it, my cupboards don't have anything to do with anything. How can we talk if you're so overwrought?"

"It makes a guy a little overwrought to get a phone call like I got. God, what would have happened if I hadn't told John you were pregnant? What if he hadn't been ready for you? Oh, God, I hate even to think—"

"Wait a minute. When did you tell John I was pregnant?"

"Over a week ago. I know you think I'm just a simpleminded preacher, but do you honestly think I'm too dumb to know how long I've been stopping at the damn drugstore? Don't you think I know what you have been waiting for? Don't you think I noticed that what you're waiting for hasn't come for over two months now? Beverly, where is your brain?"

At this moment she had absolutely no idea.

"Wait a minute. If you knew you didn't have to, why did you keep using those things?"

"Because I was giving you time. Because I thought you would have the decency and presence of mind to talk to me about the baby we made. And because you said you loved me, and I thought that meant you trusted me and that we could talk to each other. I thought you might go to John if you wouldn't come to me, but I never thought you would do what you would have done. Never. Beverly, why?"

Beverly was going to cry. It wasn't nice to scream at a brainless, pregnant woman. It would be nice to fall into the assistant minister's arms, but there was no way he was saying "come here." He was just going to stand there with his red face and glare at her. He wouldn't make a very understanding husband.

"Answer me!"

"I can't."

"Why the hell not? Don't you know why you almost did what you almost did?"

"Only sort of."

"Then sort of answer me!"

"Not until you stop yelling."

"Not until you answer me!"

"Because I love you and I didn't want you to be stuck. And because I don't want to be the minister's wife at Santa Monita. I'm not holy enough to be a preacher's wife, and the nice little congregation would snicker and whisper when they found out you had to marry the widow you were screwing around with— that's why."

"That's stupid."

Well, he wasn't yelling. But he wasn't backing down either. Beverly was going to have to do something a little more dramatic to bring him around. Or irrational. She ran out of the room and threw herself on her bed to sob. Mistake number one.

"Really stupid." He was following her. He sat on the end of the bed and muttered, "I have never heard anything so stupid."

"Well, why do you want to marry me if I'm so stupid?"

"I don't know," he said, completely exasperated.

"See." Sniff. "It would have flopped."

"Listen, the first rule is that the preacher gets to pick out his own wife. No one gets a vote. The congregation doesn't get a vote, the women's circle doesn't get a vote, and the youth council doesn't get a vote. Rule number two is they don't hire the preacher's wife; they hire the preacher. And rule number three is if they snicker, who gives a damn? Besides, I already wrote to Santa Monita and told them I couldn't come."

"You did what?"

"You heard me."

"Why?"

"Because I knew you didn't want to go with me."

"Joe. Are you crazy? The 'God trip,' remember? First before me and first before everything. What were you thinking of? I never asked you to give up anything for me."

"Oh, no. Just the three most important people in my life and the only baby I ever made. You're real generous."

"But the God thing, for gosh sakes."

"Sometimes I think your head is full of marbles, Beverly. I didn't give up God. I can keep Him forever and do His work anywhere. Do you really think I would leave you now? And the boys? I know you believe you're a terrific father for them, but they think you stink as a father. They want a real one."

"Well, if you still have all that almighty devotion, how come you were screwing around with me, huh?"

"Beverly, I made a commitment to you. Not a pretend one, a real one. I wanted to wait until you were committed back to me, but I goofed up."

"Oh, good, I'm a goof-up. Well, did you say 'Please forgive me?' Did you?"

"Yes."

"I knew you would! I knew it! Well, what did He say?"

"Oh, shit, Beverly, ask Him yourself."

"You're yelling again. And you're swearing like crazy."

"I am so damned mad, I can't see straight. I don't know when I have ever been this mad."

"Joe, listen to me, please. Go to Santa Monita and preach. I made a big mistake and I don't want you to pay for it with your career. They need you there."

"Beverly, I have been talking to you for over eight months and I don't believe you have ever heard me. I did not write that letter because you're pregnant. Before the baby, before we made love, I was committed to you. You didn't commit back, but I still did make the commitment. It was not a half-assed decision, not some little thing I said to myself to make it seem right. It was an honest-to-God commitment. I just can't live any other way. I don't want to. Beverly, you are driving me crazy. Will you please just give up and marry me?"

"I can't. I'm too scared."

"Of what?"

"Of everything. I'm going to take a long, hot bath."

"Not now. Talk to me now. Take a bath later."

"No, I'll have a good soak while you calm down, and then we'll talk."

Women. Crazy. Crazy down to the very last one. So how do you stop her from taking a bath when the water is already running? And she's starting to undress? So even after all you've done together she locks the door? When she's already pregnant, she locks the door? What's she afraid of? That you might see her naked or something?

Joe fell back on the bed and started to laugh. This whole thing was getting plain ridiculous. Now, what kind of a woman would love you and refuse to marry you when she's pregnant? Beverly. Only Beverly. And run out of booze and stop smoking and help with the youth group and attend church and go to the church alone at night to pray for strength and courage and faith and still believe she couldn't believe? Beverly. Beverly the scared and confused and lonely. So why wouldn't she just marry him and not be alone anymore and let him help her with all the other stuff? Because, Joe, that would make too much sense.

"Come on, Beverly, that's enough bathing. We have to talk."

No answer.

"Beverly?"

Nothing.

"Beverly, open this door. Right now. I mean it!"

No response.

No, God, no, she isn't that scared. Oh, God, please let her be okay. Okay, I'm begging now, please don't let Beverly be that stupid. Just this once. Please!

Joe, who was not given to panic, gave in to panic. He had had a very rough day. He jiggled the doorknob frantically and then started throwing himself against the bathroom door until the latch gave out and he went crashing into the sink. He was trying to remember how to give mouth-to-mouth resuscitation, when he saw Beverly trying to cover her breasts with the washcloth.

"What is it you're doing?" she asked.

"I was going to save your life." He sighed, sitting down on the toilet seat beside the tub. "Why didn't you answer me?"

"I didn't want to." Not scared or suicidal, just stubborn and downright bitchy at times.

"You're a real pain in the ass, Beverly."

Sniff. Sniff. "So are you."

Joe put a foot on the edge of the tub and leaned an elbow on his raised knee. He wondered if God was holding his sides by now.

"Okay, Beverly, level with me for once and tell me what you're scared of. Give it to me straight."

"You wouldn't understand."

"Why don't you try me?"

"Okay. It's bad enough when something unexpected screws up your life. But if I have the chance to protect myself and the boys, I'm going to do it. I couldn't bear it if we got married and it failed. It would hurt the boys too. It would be the end."

"I understand."

"You do?"

"Yep. But I don't understand why you think I'm so naive. I think if we're both scared that it might not work, but we love each other a lot, we'll make it work. Most of it already works. And I think you'd make a damn good minister's wife, because you're not spiritual, boring, or dull. I wouldn't drag you out to California just to break your heart. Besides, I wouldn't get mixed up with any church that turned people away, preacher's wives or regular heathens, and I think you already know that. And risk hurting the boys? You know I wouldn't."

"And what if I get used to loving you and fighting with you and sleeping with you, and then you die on me or something? I'll be in a padded cell for the rest of my life."

"Better to never love than to love and suffer loss? What are you going to do? You're close to a padded cell right now, going it alone. Look at yourself. You're a wreck."

"I'm not going to stay alone forever. Only until I can face the risk again."

"Look, it hurts when you think you're calling all the shots and some disaster comes along and screws everything up. Beverly, you're going to have to deal with it."

"I'm too scared."

"Well, tough, so am I. If I let myself think I might lose you and the boys, I don't know if I could live through it either. And what about the boys? If something happened to you, where would they be? Wouldn't you want them to be with me?"

"You'd just be stuck again."

"Oh, knock it off, Beverly, you know I love them as much as I love you. You can't fool me, you know it."

"How am I going to get over this fear?"

"A little bit at a time."

"With you?"

"I can't think it would be better alone."

"Well, you might think you want to have a baby, but—"

"Beverly, if you do anything to that baby, something inside of me is going to die. How am I going to get over that fear?"

"I don't think I could have gone through with it. I get a little irrational when I'm pregnant."

"So I've noticed."

"Well, it's no picnic living with a pregnant woman. And I'm not sure I'll be at all happy with a man who would give up his entire lifelong dream just to stick it out with the widow he knocked up. I bet you were planning a Christian home for unwed mothers, weren't you?"

"I wrote the letter. I didn't exactly mail it."

"Joseph! Isn't that kind of sneakiness a sin or something?"

"Are you going to marry me?"

"Are you going to make a pest out of yourself?"

"Yes."

"Well, I don't think your little congregation is going to be very impressed with me as a preacher's wife, but it's your funeral." She smiled sheepishly. "I couldn't have done it, you know."

"What?"

"The abortion. That was probably one of my tough acts. And I might have told you to go without me, but if you had—"

"Is that a yes?"

"Yes. Yes."

"Great. Get out of the tub. You're starting to pucker."

"I better get dressed. John will be bringing the boys home pretty soon."

"Uh-uh, he'll call first, to make sure we have things settled here. He'd keep them for a month if it took that long. But it won't."

"What?"

"I want to practice the consummation. Come on."

Fifteen

everly was often emotional, and when she was pregnant she was emotional all the time. She wouldn't have a church wedding and she was decided about that. A civil ceremony at her mother's house was as much as she would agree to, and she said when she was sure about the God thing she would say the vows with Joe in his own church; his Santa Monita Church.

That was Beverly. She wouldn't give in, but she said "when" not "if" and so Joe just smiled and said okay. He wasn't as dumb as she thought.

Beverly was as nervous as a cat all the way to California. She worried about everything. "So what are you going to tell the people if they ask when we got married?"

"Last summer. We're newlyweds."

"Swell."

"Beverly, they won't ask how new. Relax."

"So what are you going to say if they ask you when and how you asked me to marry you? Are you going to say, 'Well, she was in the bathtub and I was sitting on the toilet,' huh?"

The people at Santa Monita didn't ask any of those questions. They liked Beverly. They accepted her honesty, her humor, and even her doubts. Beverly just couldn't keep her mouth shut. But she loosened things up a lot and told them she didn't think a church should be boring or dull. She found out there were plenty of people with doubts of their own. Of course, they all loved Joe. Who wouldn't?

And Beverly learned something about people who struggled with their faith. It was very disconcerting to think of yourself as the only person who wasn't sure, but Joe, in one of his very first sermons, said that those who knew everything, who had no questions of their own, had no more mortal work to do. Unless, maybe in their perfection, their mortal work was to tolerate the questions of others and help them find their way. But he wasn't one of those, he said. He still had a lot of work to do. Leave it to Joe to say, diplomatically, that doubts and fears were little more than mortal work, or else go ahead to heaven. And he proved it by being wild about his wife, who considered herself a mess.

She might not be holy enough to be a minister's wife, but she certainly was pregnant enough, Bev thought. The time flew and she blossomed in her pregnancy and was very busy with her new husband and her new friends. And the boys thrived. They started to sound more like Joe every day.

The nice thing about being the chief reverend is not the pay, but that there is always a doctor or dentist or veterinarian in the congregation. There happened to be a friendly neighborhood ob-gyn whom Beverly liked almost as much as she did Carl. Except that he wouldn't put up with as much as Carl. Tom was tough and strict.

He said warm and understanding things like: "I don't care if you're trying to cut out the salt, you are obviously not trying hard enough. Now, would you like to go home and start really trying, or would you like to try hospital food?"

"Don't get ugly, Tom. Be nice now or I'll call the preacher in here to straighten you out."

"Call him. He had his chance last Sunday."

"Are you saying the reverend hasn't reached you?"

"He reached you and that's all I care about. He gets to put it in there and I have to take it out. And you're not making my job any easier."

Why did Beverly get herself mixed up with crabby obstetricians? Because she was wild about them. Because she was sassy and liked a good fight better than anything. If she could ever get her spirit straightened out, she would probably do some good fighting for the cause. But until then she would just fight with Tom, every week now. Beverly was ready to pop.

Bev's first really good friend was Val, the crabby ob's wife. Val wasn't any more secure than Bev, so they talked over lunch, over coffee, and, occasionally, though more rarely due to pregnancy, over a drink. The medicinal kind, scotch.

"Is Tom sure?" Bev asked.

"Yep. He says in his business the only thing he's sure of is that there is a God."

While Beverly doubted, she learned from Joe because he talked to her and never made her feel foolish. She did think it was kind of silly that the minister claimed to be learning right along with her. He should have a better handle on things. But she couldn't help falling more deeply in love with him. Deeper and stronger than she ever thought she could.

There was one night when Joe was feeling the baby move that he asked her if she would tell him some things about Bob. She couldn't understand why he would be interested. She thought he would want her to forget. It seemed he might get jealous hearing about this perfect, superhuman man whom she had adored.

"Jealous? I don't think you should try so hard to forget him. I mean, I think I should know a few things so when I talk to the boys, we can talk about their dad. Wouldn't it be great if Mark had inherited some special talent, like a good pitching arm, that was from Bob? I'd hate to think they'd forget him, even though they were pretty young. We can keep him alive a little. I think a father is a really good thing. I think if you could have two, you should."

Beverly found him remarkable. More together than any other man she had ever known. Tender, loving, warm, patient, sensible, and logical. Until the night the baby came.

"This has been hell for you, hasn't it, Joe? Admit it, you hate pregnant women."

"I love pregnant women. Come here."

"Why should I 'go there'? I can't do anything. Didn't Tom tell you I can't do anything? This baby is due, really due. I feel like shi—"

"Beverly! Not in front of your stomach!"

"I do. And my back hurts and my feet are as big as yours, and I have to go to the bathroom every two minutes. Look at me. I'm a mess."

"You're beautiful. Come here. I want to feel your belly. Now, could this big belly be anything but a miracle."

"It's a biologically natural thing."

"Yeah, sure, and we're all glad you didn't work out all the details; you're not nearly original enough. I'll rub your back if you'd like."

"No, I feel awful."

"You're okay, aren't you, baby? I mean, I know you're uncomfortable, but you're—"

"No," she snapped. "Ohhhhhhh," she groaned. She had been having little ones all day, but that was the first really good contraction. "Oh! Jeez!"

"What? What? Beverly! What?"

"Oh, calm down. Didn't you learn anything in those classes? Don't panic. I'm in labor."

Joe wasn't one to panic, only when he thought Beverly was going to kill herself or have a baby. He called Tom right away. Tom said, "That's nice," when he heard that Beverly had had one whole contraction. What kind of a doctor says something like that? One with a lot of experience, that's what kind.

Tom was cool. He said to relax and call him when the pains were five minutes apart. Then they would all meet at the hospital. There was plenty of time.

But it was nighttime. That happened occasionally. Every single day in fact. Joe would have to call somebody to stay with the boys and he would have to get Beverly into the car. What if the baby came in the car and it was dark? He would hurry up and pray, but first he would have a drink.

"Oh, no, you don't. I'm not going anywhere with you if you have a drink. You know you can't hold your liquor. Now, shape up or I'll have this baby on the couch."

"Aren't you in pain or something?"

"I'm going to be in a minute. Now, are you going to get your act together or do I call Tom and have him send Val over?"

"I'm a little nervous."

"I could tell. I'm very perceptive. I don't want to have to drive myself to the hospital. Are you going to be the coach, or are you already out?"

He got it together. Men. You'd think having a baby was some kind of sideshow.

"Okay, breathe... two... three... doing great. Relax a little more and don't tighten up."

"Very good, Joseph. Now, stay cool because this is something I like to take my time with, all right? And it's going to get a lot worse before it gets better."

"Okay, fine. Let's go now."

"No, it's too soon. I'd like a cup of coffee."

Oh, boy, Joe had heard all those stories about women who didn't think it was going to happen fast and they stopped for coffee and had their babies in diners. No diner or taxicab or subway birth for him. No sir.

"Beverly, I'm begging, okay? I'm not very good at this kind of thing and I want to go to a place where there are all kinds of doctors and nurses hanging around. Please? Please, Beverly? I might never have another baby and I really don't want to screw this up. Please?"

It was going to be a long night because the baby didn't care that Joe was in a hurry. It was going to take its old sweet time. And Tom wasn't going to come to the hospital until he had to, because Tom was smart. Joe wasn't. He was going to call Tom every few minutes to report their progress. Until Tom warned him, very nicely, that if he called again, he would leave that baby in there forever. Tom knew how to shut Joe up.

Bright-eyed and well-rested, Tom strolled into the labor room the next morning. "Well, how are we doing?"

"Oh, shut up," in unison, no less.

"Long night? Well, let's have a look here. Ah-ha. Doing fine. Just fine. Shouldn't be too much longer."

"I've been in labor forever. Whoever heard of such a thing for a third labor. What in the world is wrong with this baby? I've had it. I... oh... OH... ohhhhhhhh..."

"Okay, honey, just relax, breathe, and go with it, don't fight it now... one... two..." The voice of Joe. Low and firm. Loving. The pulpit voice. There was another voice in a labor room once. Not such a perfect pulpit voice, but just as loving. Some women don't even get one and I get two? So how come, God? Just why?

"Okay, honey, we're going to the delivery room and you can start to push when Tom is ready."

"Are you coming with me, Joe?"

He wouldn't miss it for the world. He had been waiting his whole life for this. And he was praying, of all things. Out loud. He was using absolutely no discretion and praying out loud in front of the nurses. Tom wasn't praying; he was snipping. "Ready to push?"

"No."

"You want to be pregnant forever?"

"I'll be ready in a minute. I don't have to right now. I'll push when I have to."

"I'm ready when you are," said the catcher.

"Boy, am I ready," said Joe.

Beverly pushed once. Noble effort. She gave a second, a good hard one, and delivered the baby's head. Joe was all but climbing over her to see the baby's head. He was wild, begging them to hurry. She would have laughed at him, but the urge came and she let them have it.

"Here you go, Preach," Tom said. "Looks like a little girl. Nope, not little. Fat, as a matter of fact. Good for you, Bev."

Beverly looked up into the face of her husband. "God," he whispered.

Joe had real honest tears. Overwhelmed tears. "I never did anything in my whole stupid life to deserve this. Oh, Bev, I love you so much. Oh, Lord, thank You, thank You, thank You. Beverly, thank you. You've made me the happiest man in the whole world. I was praying for a baby girl before we were even married."

"Well, that explains a lot! You idiot! What were you doing praying for a baby then? With all the influence you have? From now on you will check all your prayers with me before you pray them, do you hear? Who knows what you'll ask for next."

"I love you. I'm so happy. The boys will love her."

"You really are crying, aren't you?"

"Yep."

"Why?"

"I'm so happy. Aren't you happy, Bev?"

No, very sad, as a matter of fact. It sounded like another voice in a delivery room once, first with Mark, then with Chuckie. She couldn't block him out; he came right in. He was thrilled and in love, too, acting like Beverly was some kind of miracle herself. "Yes, Joe, very happy." So what's a little lie? You didn't want to rain on the man's parade, now, did you?

Beverly was very quiet. No one really noticed, least of all Joe. He was busy going crazy over the baby and Tom was putting in stitches. You were tired after having a baby, so you could be quiet too.

Beverly was quiet the next day and the day after. Having a baby could do that to a woman, shut her up for once. She could hold the new little life, if she could get her away from Joe, and nurse the baby at her breast. Quiet time. A good time to think and feel. Time to contemplate love and life and miracles... and memories.

Joe liked to watch her nurse the baby. He wished he could nurse the baby. She had never heard anything so ridiculous in her life—except when Bob had said the very same thing.

Joe simmered down from wild excitement to a sort of plain brilliance. He was in love. He wanted to know if they could name the baby Allison May, in memory of his sister. She said maybe they could if he would promise not to call her "Al." He wasn't sure he could promise, because the boys were already calling her that. They were already crazy about her too.

Joe allowed Beverly to be quiet without worrying about her. He had a long talk with a really good Friend. He knew what was happening to Beverly; he hoped she wasn't going to change. He liked her sassy; he liked her irreverent. Beverly was made a certain way for a certain reason, and he loved her so much. He told his Friend, his Father, and asked if Beverly wasn't pretty terrific? Then he waited very patiently for an answer that he didn't quite need. He had never felt so good, so sure, in all his life. Those kind of answers were perfectly acceptable. Joe was not the burning-bush type.

The day came for Bev to take "Al" home. She had three days of deep thought and silence and now it was time to get her act together, go home, and be the preacher's wife again.

Beverly was dressed and ready, discharged and waiting for the preacher to show up. She would have another hour to wait, so she asked the nursery nurse if it was all right to use that time to go to the hospital chapel. It was probably the last free sitter she would ever get.

It was dimly lit and small. Not scary like the last time. But she lit candles anyway; one of the first things she was going to do was turn the non-Catholics on to this candle lighting jazz. It really did help.

Okay, God, I'm here. I want an immediate hold on all miracles. I'm not sure I can take anymore. I suppose You think I didn't notice. Well, it took a while, but I see it now. Believe me, had I known You were that serious, I would have paid more attention. You didn't waste any troops: John, Mother, Terry, Joe,

Carl, and finally a whole church full of them. My own sons and my dear, sweet Bob. A great big real-life play, or is that plan? And having me drag Joe off to bed like a nymphomaniac, now, really. Forget it, I know. Allison.

So it's like this. Lord, I'm catching on. When You mean business, You don't fool around. So before you call in the National Guard, I give up. I don't want You to think this is going to be easy. I have a lot of questions, a lot of confusion. But I do believe in You. I may not understand, but I believe. So please, I will stop fighting if You will stop the miracles while I catch my breath. Is that good enough? I surrender.

Bev felt a presence in the chapel. This time she knew it wasn't the hand of God on her shoulder, she could feel that somewhere else. This particular person had a reputation for hanging out in churches, and his aftershave was extremely familiar. But Bev didn't turn around to look at him. She had business at hand, personal business. And she knew she wasn't finished. She was beginning.

And remember, Lord, when I talked to You about Joe? I told You I could never love that much again. I didn't even want to. I was wrong about a lot of things, and that was one of them. I'm beginning to see it all now. I never would have believed that so much love would come out of so much pain. I guess I wasn't the only one to come into this marriage with a package deal. Thanks. I really mean it. Thanks. A lot.

A little voice in the back of the heart, or soul, or mind said: "Anytime."

About The Author

I was born and raised in St. Paul, Minnesota in the midst of a large, closely-knit, noisy, nosey family. I married the man I had dated through high school and college, and proceeded to follow him around the United States while he pursued a military flying career.

In 1975, with a one-year-old hanging on my legs and a second child due to be born any second, I began writing a novel. The transition was so startling, I was probably as surprised as anyone. In the early days, typing on the dining room table while children crawled around my feet, I embraced the family legacy of telling all.

The kids are older now, and rather than changing diapers and pushing strollers, I drive carpools and write checks. We don't move every year, and I have my own room in which to type. But the feelings I get from storytelling are the same: exhilaration, satisfaction, joy.

Every writer has had the "spooky" experience of having a story hit the page with such spontaneity that it seemed to write itself. In a dozen years, every book I've written has had stages when that seemed the case, but when Beverly and Joe started to work through their relationship, I began to feel more like an observer than a creator. That is only one of the reasons they're so special to me.

—Robyn Carr

Robyn Carr is a RITA Award-winning, #1 New York Times bestselling author of fifty novels, including the critically acclaimed Virgin River series. Her new series, Thunder Point, made its debut as a #1 NYT bestseller in March 2013. Robyn and her husband live in Las Vegas, Nevada. You can visit Robyn Carr's website at www.RobynCarr.com or follow her on Twitter at @RCarrWriter.

Here's a sneak peek at Robyn's romantic suspense novel:

Mind Tryst

Chapter One

The truth matters. To my mind the first symptom of evil or derangement exists in the lie. How evil, how deranged depends on the magnitude of the lies. I think of that as I look around my house, partially remodeled, filled with boxes packed for moving. Again. I've been here a year. It took a year for the lies to build to a climax that could have cost me my life.

In my work, in family law, I expect exaggerations. I expect an extraordinary bias. Clients do not admit that they're jealous of their ex-spouse's new partner as they ask to change the custodial guardianship or visitation. I have never had a client confess that he or she is molesting the child. I sometimes rely on gut feelings.

I have been heard to preach on the subject of lies, especially to my son, Sheffie, who has been dead three years now. He was only eleven when I lost him; he stays an eleven-year-old in my dreams and imagination, though I desire to imagine him at fourteen. I would say things like, "You cannot know the power of a lie, no matter how small. And 'If it isn't the whole truth, it's a lie.'"

When I moved here to this small Colorado town, to practice family law, one of the first things I did was consider the creation of a partial lie. I came to work for and with Roberta Musetta, a sixty-year-old attorney who had practiced in this town for thirty years. I was willing for Roberta to know the details of my personal life but was not willing for everyone to know everything. "Let's say never married, no children."

She looked at me levelly, her brown eyes hovering over the rim of her glasses. "I think I can understand the 'no children,' but why 'never married'?"

"I was only married for a year, Sheppard is my maiden name, and often when I say I am divorced people feel compelled to ask me if I have children. It's painful for me to say that I had a son and he is dead. It's a kindness, if you think about it, because no one knows what to say next. No one."

"How did he die?" she asked.

"Or they say that."

Roberta was not intimidated by anything and she hadn't been then, either. I could be so damned defensive about it sometimes. "He was on his bike in an intersection and was hit by an armored car. Witnesses said he was crossing against the light. He died instantly. He was eleven."

"I'm sorry for your loss."

"Thank you, Roberta. I can talk about it; it's talking about it with everybody that bothers me. One of the reasons I've come here is for a complete change of scenery, lifestyle, a new beginning. When a single mother loses an only child, there is a devastating kind of aloneness. It terrifies people and makes them behave more strangely than the bereaved. I couldn't deal with the reaction anymore."

"I see," Roberta said. But she couldn't come close without the details. The zenith of the events was when a close friend, Chelsea, broke into my house when I refused to answer the phone and door one Saturday for reasons that had nothing to do with grief. I was avoiding a man determined to date me, I'd had a brutal week in court, I had drunk too much the night before and had a vicious headache, and I wasn't expecting anyone. I unplugged my answering machine and phone so I wouldn't be tempted. I turned up the stereo so I could hear it all the way to the bathroom and filled up the tub. The loud music drowned out the doorbell. I thought about gardening later; I thought of trying a good book. Imagine my delight when a young policeman entered my bathroom with my friend.

I can't criticize Chelsea; she is a dedicated caretaker. I had been depressed, overworked, and impatient; I had not left my answering machine on, my car was in the garage, and the stereo was blasting. Clearly I had hanged myself or taken an overdose of pills.

I was determined to change things. I couldn't stand the pity and I couldn't stand being watched so carefully.

"I shouldn't ask you to lie for me," I had said to Roberta. "I suppose I could try changing the subject or refusing to answer."

"It'll be over quicker," Roberta replied, "if you just say to anyone else what you said to me. I, for one, am unwilling to elaborate on the personal lives of friends and coworkers."

A part of me embraced what she said. Speaking of Sheffie's death caused me pain, but his life had given me great joy. By erasing him, I would rob myself of that pleasure. He lived in my heart and mind; I couldn't wish him away with a lie. Not even to save myself from some pain. Still, another part of me held reservations about revealing too much too soon.

My task, in telling what happened to me here in Coleman, is to explain how a woman sensitive to liars, experienced in dealing with them, and intelligent, can end up in grave danger. End up nearly dead. My sanity abandoned me; my clear head, steady hand, and sound instincts were buried under an avalanche of lies and manipulations. For a while I couldn't distinguish between the rational and irrational.

It's easy to find the beginning. I was sitting right here, in this room, on this curved white sofa. My knee was raised, as it is now, and I held a cup of coffee with both hands. The bookshelves were not there and the walls weren't painted. There were boxes scattered around the room because I didn't have the strength to unpack. I was depressed, and surprised to be. I had made a major change in my circumstances, and all the while I prepared to leave Los Angeles, I had been excited and optimistic for the first time in years.

I had traveled to Coleman several times. A sleepy old mining and lumber town southwest of Denver, it's in a pleasant valley with no highway. There is little mining now and timber is seasonal work; there's ranching, some farming, hunting, camping, skiing, tourism. Coleman is one of several small towns nestled in what is called the Wet Mountain Valley; there's the Silver Springs Bar and Restaurant, a refurbished hotel that's one hundred and twenty years old, some raised sidewalks, and an old scenic-rail service.

The town has been rediscovered by the baby boomers; young professionals who have opted to trade materialism for an atmosphere of safety and tranquility have come here. You can get your teeth crowned cheap — we have several young dentists. In the past fifteen years, I'd been told, the town had sprouted some bed-and-breakfast inns, an herb-tea manufacturer, organic farmers, and even a women's shelter. The population is under one thousand, with another thousand in surrounding rural areas who would claim Coleman as their town. It's one of the bigger unincorporated towns that speckle the large valley. Pueblo is the closest city, with a population of forty thousand. Denver and Colorado Springs are not out of reach to anyone willing to make the one-to two-hour drive. Most of our services — sheriff, hospital, social services, et cetera — come from the Henderson County seat in Pleasure, some thirty miles up the road. Coleman does have its own fire truck and ambulance now, with an active volunteer fire department and auxiliary. There's a great high-school football team, a major real-estate conglomerate, and a charming combination of the old and the new.

Since I had somehow managed to buy a newly built tract house in Southern California, I chose a house in Coleman that was sixty years old. I was doing everything differently. I hoped to do much of the renovation of this old house myself.

That day that comes to mind found me immobilized by depression. I had suddenly felt as though I had abandoned my son by leaving L.A. He had been dead two years already, but he was so much on my mind that I couldn't function. I couldn't unpack the boxes, put on my makeup, or make conversation. I had hired someone Roberta suggested could help me, a handyman-builder by the name of Tom Wahl. He was an average-looking, not unhandsome, friendly man. He had dark-brown hair, brown eyes and a nose with a bony bump on its bridge. Like most men who did heavy work, he had large, callused hands and strong shoulders. He wasn't a great big guy, five ten or so, with a rather thick torso. He measured my wall for shelves, making small talk about how much personality these old houses had — each one different — and I looked as though I should be put to bed.

I was preoccupied, sitting on the curving sofa I'd been so proud of, wishing I had sold it along with the other things I had decided to leave behind. I had saved for two years to buy it, and because of its white, sterile appearance, I kept it covered so Sheffie wouldn't soil it. What I was remembering was the number of nights he had fallen asleep on it and I had either carried him or directed him sleepily to his bed. Damn. It could happen to me like that, without provocation. I didn't need a photo or favorite toy to be jarred into that sense of loss. I was overcome with longing for my child. There were times I thought I was doing so well; then other times I thought I'd never recover.

Add to that the fact that I've never had a robust appearance. Up until Sheffie died my friends would claim to be jealous of the fact that stress takes weight off me rather than induces me to eat and plump out. I have one of those pale, anemic complexions — if I cry briefly, I look as though I've cried for days. The suggestion of tears causes the rims of my eyes to become red, my nose gets watery and pink, and I splotch. I get hives and rashes easily. My hair is strawberry blond, enhanced by a rinse which became my prerogative at thirty-seven when I arrived in Coleman. Sitting there in old wrinkled clothes, holding coffee, looking pink around the gills, and being in that dismal, remote mood, I must have given Tom the impression I was a sad case.

"Miss Sheppard?" he asked. "Who, ah, painted that wall?"

"I did," I said defensively. I remembered thinking that anyone can paint a wall. Not true. I had made it look far worse than it had — streaked and gloppy. It looked like a window that had been cleaned with a wet paper towel that only smeared the dirt around.

"It could use a little touching up, don't you think?"

I looked away from the wall, not answering. It was a stupid question.

"I could paint it for you," he suggested.

"No, thanks. For right now let's just stick to the shelves."

"I wasn't going to charge you."

That always gets my attention. I am suspicious of freebies. "Why would you do that?"

"Well, you'd have to buy the paint. You need primer, too. I could write it down for you, tell you what to get."

"But why?"

"Why not? I have the time and it looks like you could use the help. Roberta says you're planning to do extensive work on the house."

I have no trouble getting right to the point. "So, you would paint that wall for me and then I would be sure to call you when I'm ready to start on the kitchen and bathrooms?"

He was scribbling a measurement on his white notepad. When he had finished, he looked at me and laughed. "I don't care whether you call me or not, Jackie. I don't need the work. I was just trying to help."

"And I'm just trying to find out why." I was sounding more and more difficult, more and more bitchy. It was as if I was challenging him: *Don't try to like me; I won't be liked.* But it was more than that; I knew there had to be a straight answer in there somewhere.

"Because you're going to have to call someone; it appears you can't do it. And you look worn out. And you're a friend of Roberta's, who is a friend of mine. Though you might not be used to it, the people in this town help each other out when they can. The permanents, anyway. Where are you from?"

"Los Angeles."

His tape measure sang as he extended it. "That explains it."

"Oh?"

"L.A. is a different kind of place. I lived there for a few years myself. This kind of thing never happens in L.A. At least not without a catch. It happens all the time here."

"What did you do in L.A.?" I asked. I know I asked that right away and I also know that he didn't give a sign of being uncomfortable with the question.

"Paperwork," he said, his back to me. "And I never liked it. I'm from the Midwest... suburb of Chicago. After a few years in Los Angeles I started looking for places outside of the city where I could get out of the smog and noise. I had tried northern California, Oregon, Washington, and it ended up I fell in love with Colorado. I don't ski; I like to camp, hike, fish... I like it better in summer — one year I bought some land. I started to build on it, and without any concrete plans to, I had settled here." He said all this while he was measuring. And writing numbers down.

"We can put some shelves around the fireplace, like so," he said, gesturing with one hand. "I think you'd like the look if I removed this old oak mantel and replaced it with bleached pine like the shelves. Let me draw you a picture first. Then I'll write up a materials list and estimate."

"What did you do in Los Angeles?" I asked again, relentless as a typical litigator.

"I wasn't a carpenter, that's for sure. Everything in L.A. is prefab. I worked for the state in the social services department. Becoming a carpenter by trade was an accident. When I came out here permanently and started building my house, I met everyone connected with selling me my supplies and people started paying me to help them with their building and woodworking."

"Social services," I said. "I'm in family law."

"Really? Oh, wow," he said, laughing. "You're a lawyer?"

"Yes."

He laughed some more. "Figures."

"Figures, how?"

"Oh, I feel embarrassed for myself. Roberta told me you'd be working in her office, and being the male chauvinist I am, I figured you were a secretary. Sorry," he added sheepishly. "Even with Roberta being here most of her life, some of us are still not used to women lawyers, women doctors, and that." The "and that" was pure Chicago, a regional speech habit like the "ay?" of Canadians. He put his pencil in the pocket of his plaid flannel shirt. "Good for you," he said.

I tend to forgive people like carpenters for having sexist notions and am impressed when a laborer knows that much about his values and conditioning. I'm easily charmed by men who seem to want to be better men.

"I'll make a drawing for you. It'll take me a few days."

"Thanks," I told him, following him to the door.

I didn't think about him again that week, except for the fleeting thought that this was a nice guy. The town, in fact, seemed dominated by nice men. I met some in the office — Roberta making introductions — or in this or that store. Those who hadn't been introduced nodded on the street. The school crossing guards waved; the postman always had time to chat.

That first week in Coleman it took all my energy to behave as though I weren't deeply troubled by thoughts of Sheffie. First the sight of the sofa filled me with memories that made me cry. Next, as I was looking at that damned wall, I remembered part of an argument we had when he colored on the wallpaper. He'd been a good kid, never before did things like that, and it was a milestone of mine — wallpaper.

Do you know how much this wallpaper cost? How I had to scrimp to buy it?

I didn't mean to.

You did mean to; you had to mean to — you did it.

He had gotten one of his rare spankings then. I had cried as I stripped off a section of wallpaper and replaced it. I found I could afford the time and expense of the repair; I had overreacted. In those pre-child support, post-law school days, I had indulged in so few luxuries and held each one dear.

I have an ex-husband, Mike. I have to struggle to remember how it was I accidentally married him. Those reasons wouldn't snag me now: He was reckless, sexy, and somewhat arrogant. I was right out of college when we met. He was in his second year of college after four years in the Air Force as an enlisted man. In retrospect, he wasn't even a particularly good date, much less husband. He had been an awful husband — inattentive, self-centered, restless. He was going to school on the G.I. Bill; I was working as a secretary in a law office, hoping to train as a paralegal. My income was not enough to support us, and Mike had to work part-time in addition to school.

His name is Michael Alexander, and he began to step out on me, I suspect, in the first three months we were married. I didn't know it at the time, of course. I began to suspect him of affairs, if not just carousing, before our anniversary.

We argued constantly, didn't like any of the same things or people, couldn't agree on room temperature, lighting requirements, or television shows. After three or four months I began to have dinner out with my friends and he went to sporting events or played poker with his. We accomplished one amiable discussion in our marriage, about our divorce.

One Saturday, when I was cleaning and doing laundry and he was working on a paper for school while simultaneously watching a football game, I said to him, "It just isn't working, is it?"

He stared at me for a minute, got up and turned off the TV for the first time since we'd married, and then said, "No, Jack, I guess it isn't working." He is the only person who ever called me Jack.

"Maybe we ought to talk about ending it rather than fight about who's right and who's wrong."

And we had. We were far more civilized in our divorce than we had ever been in marriage. It seemed we'd finally found something we could do together amicably. The little house we occupied was leased and I could afford the rent, utilities, car payment, and insurance for at least the rest of the year without alimony. Mike had friends he could move in with.

Alimony had not occurred to me; he was a starving student. We agreed to separate and divorce sans war; we hadn't had a good time together anyway. Parting was the only thing we did that made sense.

I was twenty-three at the time. Now that I'm older, I realize how many times I have liked someone without loving him, or loved without liking. Mike I had briefly loved. I didn't like anything about him. Now, though I'm not in love with him, I'm growing to like him. He has become admirable in my eyes.

We separated and I felt instant relief. Then I missed a period. Then two. My pregnancy was a complete accident that resulted from one of our rare sexual encounters.

My fear at the time was that he'd demand to move back in and stop the divorce proceedings. Or insist I have an abortion. Although I doubted the soundness of my decision, I had instantly decided I would have my child and raise him. My reasons were murky; I wasn't sure this sort of thing would happen to me again. I hadn't dated extensively; I didn't have my sights set on love, marriage, and family. I was solitary, a trait of only children, and independent. I had learned I couldn't live with Mike Alexander, but I was certain I could live with his child.

As self-centered as he was in those days, he let me have my way as long as it didn't cost him anything. I called him from the hospital the day after Sheffie was born, and despite the fact that my parents were enormously rude to him, he was civil and thanked me for letting him look at his son. He asked if he could visit him once in a while and I said sure.

"I'm naming him Sheppard Michael Alexander," I said. "I'm going to have my maiden name again. He will be Sheppard Alexander and I will be Jacqueline Sheppard." He thanked me for giving the baby his name. Mike visited twice that first year, if I remember.

I was lonely in those first few months after Sheffie was born, but I loved him so devotedly and felt so needed that I didn't indulge the self-pity.

Years of building myself up into my idea of success followed Sheffie's birth. I moved back in with my parents to save money and have my mom's help with the baby. I worked ferociously and ambitiously. After three years with the firm and a two-year-old child, I managed to get a scholarship to law school. Why settle for being a paralegal when I was smart enough to pass the bar?

I was completely unprepared for the demands of law school, though I had been warned by the attorneys in the firm I had worked for. The constant encouragement and even tutoring from lawyers I had once typed for helped me get through. They let me clerk in the summers and offered me my first job when I passed the bar. There I was, a brand-new, freckle-faced, single-mother lawyer with a five-year old son. I was back out on my own, settled with my child in a little tract house, practicing law.

I was one of those late babies; my mother was over thirty-five when I came along and my father was older still. I had only a year in the firm when my mom, then sixty-five years old, had a heart attack and died. Her death devastated me; there were no brothers or sisters, and my father, twelve years older than my mother, was not well. We had always expected to lose him first. In addition to dealing with my loss, I had to begin to take care of my father. Had I not had Sheffie, I might have crumbled. The arms of a small, loving child can do more than penicillin for what ails you.

This is when Michael Alexander came back into my life as, get this, a model ex-husband. He had remarried, a woman named Chelsea whom I would eventually choose for a best friend even with Mike betwixt us. Chelsea was ideal for us both. She quickly gave him two daughters and pushed him back into his son's life, child support and all. He couldn't be argued into back support, but he became generous with his time and his money.

I remember that Sheffie was stunned at first, and suspicious. He soon settled into the weekend routine, which gave us both something good. Sheffie, who was losing his grandpa, had a dad, and I had valuable time to myself. I owe Chelsea. It was Chelsea's doing that Mike and I were able to forge a friendship that came as a minor relief when our son died. Mike told me it was Chelsea who said to her husband, "What do you mean you're not paying any child support? Is that how you plan to demonstrate responsibility to our daughters? And what about their right to know their brother?"

Chelsea Alexander made of Mike something I could not have managed. She somehow found potential in this playful jerk; she encouraged his dreams, his performance, his fidelity. He had majored in criminology, and became a cop. He developed a more sensitive nature because of Chelsea, fathering daughters, and working with women. His partner, I learned by accident, was a woman. I never would have fallen in love with him, but I began to respect him. I do respect him. I owe him my life. Regardless of what all the pop-psych books say — that it is impossible to change another person — Chelsea fixed Mike. She entered his life and molded him into a husband and family man. Somehow he had reached an age and maturity to know a valuable woman when he had one — and Chelsea was it.

All these things and people combined to bring me here. My father, who suffered from hardening of the arteries, was diagnosed as having that tragic thief of the mind, Alzheimer's. He had to be placed in a nursing home, and when Sheffie was killed, Dad wasn't able to comprehend it. My father was the last thread that tied me to Los Angeles. When he died it was time, I thought, for a big change. I had come to realize that I would always be plagued by a certain sadness from my losses, but in a new town I needn't be reminded by friends and acquaintances that I had once been so positive.

I set about making new friends. In a place like Coleman, a small-town civility abounds, yet conceals standoffishness. At first glance it appears friendship will be easy. I found a group of men who had coffee and cigarettes every morning at the cafe; after stopping there for a muffin-to-go three days in a row, I had become a regular and one of their acquaintances. I purposely lingered to stretch the truth with them every day. Two ranchers, a telephone lineman, a county surveyor, the hardware-store owner, and Harry Musetta, Roberta's husband. They seemed to enjoy teasing me about the time — all of eight thirty A.M. — and the fact that they had already worked half a day.

That was where I first met Billy Valenzuela, a forty-five year old man who had suffered brain damage in an auto accident when he was in his late twenties. From the time he had recovered enough to begin to function, town people gave him little jobs like yard work, dog sitting, deliveries. He was sweet and shy and had the mental capacity of a ten-year old. He was large — six feet and two hundred pounds — with a kind and gentle disposition. He drove around town in his beat-up old pickup with his dog, Lucy, and he lived alone at the edge of town in a tiny two-room house that he had shared with his mother until her death. Now the town took care of Billy, in a way, keeping him in enough cash to get by.

One morning in the cafe I ran into Tom Wahl while I was getting my muffin. He was not sitting at the long table with the men; he seemed to be adjacent to them, at his own table talking to one of the guys on the end. As if I were being reacquainted with an old friend, I gave him a big hello.

"You should watch the company you keep, Tom. These old liars are going to get you into trouble," I teased.

"Lady lawyers," Harry said, "are what get you into trouble. You can trust me on that one."

"Roberta files her briefs at work, washes Harry's briefs at home," someone joked.

"I wash all the briefs," Harry said. "They call it retirement," he added.

"I'm hanging around here waiting for you," Tom said. "I have that drawing and materials list."

"Great," I said. He passed an envelope to me and I slid it into my purse.

"Think you'll have time to look it over this morning?" he asked.

"Sure. Can I call you later?"

"I don't know where I'll be today. If I am around home, I might have the saw or drill running. I'll call you."

From that point on, I guess, I thought about Tom most of the time. And will, I suppose, for the rest of my life.

End of Sample

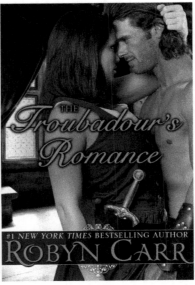

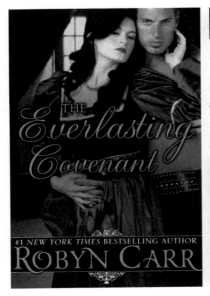

"She has done it again. Robyn Carr is absolutely marvelous."
—Danielle Steel

"Adventure, danger, derring-do, as well as doings at the glittering anything-goes court of Charles II...Carr tells an entertaining yarn." —Publishers Weekly

CPSIA information can be obtained
at www.ICGtesting.com
Printed in the USA
LVHW04s2258230418
574628LV00024B/1072/P